DEATH BECOMES HER

DEATH BECOMES HER

THE KURTHERIAN GAMBIT™ BOOK 1

MICHAEL ANDERLE

LMBPN Publishing
PMB 196, 2540 South Maryland Pkwy
Las Vegas, NV 89109

Version 2.55 February 2023
eBook ISBN: 978-1-64202-002-1

DEATH BECOMES HER TEAM

Thanks to the JIT Readers for this version

Daniel Weigert
Robert Brooks
Jackey Hankard-Brodie
Peter Manis
Jeff Eaton
Diane L. Smith
Joshua Ahles
Dorothy Lloyd
Dave Hicks
Crystal Wren
Micky Cocker
Misty Roa
Jeff Goode
Shari Regan

If I've missed anyone, please let me know!

Editor
Lynne Stiegler

To my Family:
my wife Judith,
my sons Joshua, Jacob & Joseph
my parents & my siblings.

I appreciate your love, your
support and acceptance
when you don't have a
clue what I'm talking about!

CHAPTER ONE

"May those who fight have honor, else we are doomed in the end."
—*Unknown politician's stump speech.*

"You know the problem with honor? Honor can be a restraining bitch. I've decided honor was for the *last* generation."
—*Bethany Anne Reynolds, Queen of the UnknownWorld*

Virginia, USA

The large agent cautiously entered the dilapidated wooden warehouse in old-town Virginia. Taking up most of a city block and surrounded by old weather-beaten and rusting pipes, it was an eyesore to everyone walking or driving by it.

He spoke into his mic. "Carl, three heartbeats. Smells are incredibly pungent, with a slightly sick note—kind of like they're going through severe body issues, or eating lots of yellow curry. I'm not sure which."

Carl retorted over the earpiece. "Bill, for the record, Indian food is magnificent. Your culinary bigotry is showing."

"Easy for you to say. I'm the one who has to smell it when you go overboard eating it." The agent stopped talking and silently squeezed his too-big body through holes which certainly were too small.

"Okay, I'm inside the perimeter and will be making contact inside thirty. That is three–zero seconds. Smells include heavy bleach and a subtle aroma of aforementioned nastiness. Still three tangos, no heartbeat warnings, no talking."

Carl was viewing the video feed coming from the needle camera attached to Bill's heavy helmet and mask. While there was no way Carl could ever make it on a takedown, he certainly enjoyed sitting in on the real-time action.

"Okay, big guy, I have all the info coming in from the sensors outside. We have no movement and nothing out of the ordinary. We don't seem to have any issues with flanking, so you are a go from this side. Your call, Billy Boy."

Bill swore to himself. If there was one thing that had gotten under his skin more in the last fifteen years of working with Carl other than being called "Billy Boy," he didn't know what it was. One of these days he was going to give Carl the monumental wedgie he had been asking for all that time—except he never said it when Bill was with him, and Bill never thought about it except at times like this.

One of these days, though, God help him—and the Big Guy *would* be upset—he was going to make it so Carl had to be surgically removed from his shorts.

Time to get back to business.

"Okay, have visual. Three contacts dressed in jeans and shirts, nothing different except two have hunting vests on. One has his off and is messing with it. Can't see what he's doing, since his back is to me."

At that moment, one of the men cocked his head and gestured at the other two. They suddenly looked in Bill's direction.

"You've been made, loudmouth." Carl couldn't keep the concern out of his playful jibe.

"Shit. Okay, this might get bloody. Talk to Primary and let him know we might need cleanup."

"Primary is already in listen-only mode. I'm sure he's setting up dispatches already."

The three guys around the card table stood up and fanned out, ready to take Bill on.

He sighed. It wasn't as if he was worried. He had taken down so many people in fights like this or gunfights that it wasn't even funny. While he looked about thirty-eight, he was closer to seventy-six years old. Pretty young for a vampire, actually.

While bullets hurt, he *would* mend—and the pain would remind him not to get sloppy next time.

Bill stood up, all six-foot-four of him, and confidently strode toward the three guys, stopping about ten feet away.

Damn if that smell wasn't peculiar. It bothered him. The bleach was causing his nose severe issues, but he could still smell something over the chlorine.

Carl watched through the video link as Bill asked the guys if they would like to come quietly or...

He never got out the next word. All three rushed Bill...and the signal from his headgear suddenly stopped.

The incoming video from a couple of the cameras outside that weren't damaged showed the whole wooden warehouse go up in flames while smoking embers rained from the sky onto nearby buildings. Carl was pretty sure that in seconds there wouldn't be anything left of the engulfed warehouse.

His best friend and partner had just vanished in a big ball of superheated ferocity. Carl just stared at the screens, willing Bill to come running back out through the flames.

Someone had known they were coming, and they knew how to take a vamp down. Three of them took their own lives to make it happen.

The color, what little was left, drained from Carl's face. The shock of losing his friend and being so mistaken about Bill's safety left Carl staring numbly at the screen.

The ringing of the phone broke through his pain and stupor. It was the primary contact.

He hit the talk button. "Yeah?" His voice was barely a whisper.

A gruff voice from the other end of the line began, "Tell me he has enough parts left to make it back to us, Carl." Frank was their primary contact with the government. His solo career deep in the bowels of the darkest areas of security predated Carl by decades. "I have Spec-Ops ready to extract in five minutes."

"No, Frank. We've lost him—*all* of him. I just lost my fucking best friend." Carl wanted to stab the button and terminate the call as anger and anguish directed both at those who had killed Bill and at himself boiled. "We can't afford notice right now. We're obviously being watched, and something is so rotten in Denmark I can't even think straight."

"I'm so sorry, Carl." Frank knew there wasn't much he could say. Carl was his third contact on the other side of the "red line," but this was Carl's first loss. Frank had interacted with the agents, but he was uncomfortable around them.

Frank knew that no matter what the protocol said, it was not "his program."

"What's our next step, kid?" Frank had to get Carl thinking again. Carl wasn't young, but compared to Frank's near-century mark his years were a drop in the bucket.

"Step?" Carl repeated blankly, his mind idling. The take from the outside cameras showed the warehouse burning, and there were sirens in the distance.

Probably Frank's work.

As much as Carl wanted to yell and scream or cry and drink himself into oblivion, there could be only one response.

With his voice just starting to come back, Carl replied, *"Do?*

Frank, there is only one choice. I have to wake *him* up." *Oh my God,* he thought. *What's going to happen now?*

Frank, hundreds of miles away, had much the same thought—except his was more concise.

It was simply, "Oh shit."

Washington, DC

Bethany Anne Reynolds was a sight to behold. As she proceeded down the hall of "spook central," she received surreptitious glances from a couple of the guys.

Although her hair was jet-black, her personality came straight from a redhead at the best of times.

The ones who were smart forced their gazes away instead of watching her walk down the hall. The view was not worth the scathing look they would get should Bethany Anne notice their interest.

Or the ass-kicking during a martial arts workout later. She was only five-foot-three, and that gave most of the guys a significant height and reach advantage. She had a long upper torso and her legs were a little short for her height, so she tended to wear higher heels to compensate.

It was obvious she was angry, and when Bethany Anne was angry, her better nature took a sabbatical. While she might apologize later, it was better not to risk the twins in the first place.

Some guys never understood the danger or decided just to chance watching the agent go down the hall. No matter how many HR training classes on appropriate behavior some guys took, it never overcame their natural predilection to be asses.

Today, however, was their lucky day. She didn't glance in anyone's direction, just strode down the corridor in a carefully-tailored and expensive dark suit. She had a piece of paper in her hand, and her blue eyes were flashing a warning to keep the hell away.

MICHAEL ANDERLE

It worked.

Martin Brennan, her boss (or at least her advisor, no matter what the org chart said) for the last five years, heard her coming from thirty feet away. There was no mistaking those very loud, very determined footfalls.

He sighed. It wasn't like this had been his plan. He loved her like a daughter—and just like fathering a teenager, he was about to get ripped for something he'd had nothing to do with.

This discussion was so going to suck.

Military Base, Colorado

The klaxon was sounding somewhere way in the back past all the pipes, and Matthew Wainright was getting very annoyed that apparently it had become his shit duty to go and see about it.

He had been relegated to this out-of-the-way floor deep underground some three days ago to deal with some of the really antique and really useless scientific equipment from the war—not even from recent decades. This equipment was the serious relic-style 1940s stuff.

He felt like he was doing research on the Philadelphia Experiment and had somehow pulled the shortest straw.

To top off his growing frustration with dust, grease, faded pencil-covered forms, and boxes full of useless crap, he had to be the one on duty when some fuse finally shorted and the stupid klaxon started up.

God hated him. He really did.

With disgust, he dropped the handfuls of old paperwork he was digging through in the box on the old gray metal workbench that had seen better centuries.

Time to go through Junkyard City and beat some sense into something that really shouldn't have been built this robustly, he thought.

Matthew grabbed a huge flashlight and a heavy wrench and

started traversing the lanes created by the pipes that ran every-where. Sometimes it felt like he was in the oversized engine room of a battleship rather than beneath hundreds of feet of rock in the mountains in Colorado.

Next time he talked with his parents, he was going to let them know the recruiter's promises about "seeing the world" should have conjured up thoughts of seeing the Earth's sphincter rather than Europe.

Although the buzzing from the old fluorescent fixtures couldn't be heard over the klaxon, the crappy light they produced let him see well enough. He had gone down two lanes so far, only to have to backtrack because they were dead-ends.

He was able to snake between two pipes and get onto a path with yellow stripes on the edges and a red line down the middle.

Huh, he thought, I've never seen any lanes with red lines.

Since it led in the direction of the noise, he decided it would be easiest to take the path of least resistance.

General Lance Reynolds, Base Commander, was talking with his secretary Patricia when his phone lit up on a landline from inside the base.

She reached across the desk and picked it up before he could so much as bat an eye...or appreciate the view.

Damn, but he was getting slow in his old age.

"General's office, state your case." She was ever so not-by-the-book. But if efficiency had a middle name it was "Patricia," so he didn't push the issue.

"Klaxon, uh-huh, Level Five, right. Won't shut off. Yes, I can hear it. I'm surprised you have a working phone down there. Wait, say that again? The door was opening when you arrived? Yes, it's right outside the door. I get that. It's hurting my ears right now."

"There's an envelope attached? Mmmhmm. I'll let him know. Right, you won't touch anything."

She hung up, and Lance raised an eyebrow.

"Seems like we have a little shakeup down on Five. We have an old-time vault that suddenly activated, with an envelope attached to the inside of the door. It's addressed, 'To the Base Commander.'"

Lance continued the single raised eyebrow, but she said nothing more. *Damn, that used to work.*

He sighed. "Okay, what else?"

She seemed confused. "It says, 'On your Honor,' sir."

Washington, DC

Bethany Anne rapped on the door and waited half a second before barging into Martin's office, face red and eyes furious.

He put up a hand to forestall her bitching. "Close the door without breaking it, and I'm not at fault." He had chosen this particular order for the two phrases because he didn't want to replace the glass...again.

The last time hadn't been Bethany Anne's fault, but he was sure her previous efforts to reduce his glass to shards had been.

After a significant effort to restrain her desire to slam the door, Bethany Anne turned back around and didn't give Martin a chance to get a word in edgewise. "What is the meaning of this? I have a few months, *a few months*, Martin, to finish my cases, and dammit, I can! There is *no* proof I've only got six months left to live. That's only the doc's best guess. Otherwise, I am *fine*. Nothing even comes back on any of the physicals. I'm doing better, if anything! Who made this bullshit request and took my case and shipped me out?"

Martin waited for a second to see if she was done.

"Well?"

Apparently, she was.

Martin squared his jaw and said the three words that were sure to fuel the flames of her ire.

"I don't know."

He stared at her, and she glared back at him. He could see the logic synapses firing in her brain.

If anything, she was the brightest he had. Hell, the brightest he'd ever *known*. If he could have had just a few more years with her in the field, there was no telling how many cases she would have closed.

As it was, Mother Nature was being a real black-hearted bitch. Bethany Anne had a very rare blood disease, one they hadn't even had the ability to check for until recently. The doctors, although not a hundred percent sure, pretty much agreed she had less than six months to live.

With her only twenty-eight years old, it was a crying shame. Martin admitted doing a little crying himself when no one was looking.

Besides the physicians, he was the only other soul who knew.

She hadn't even told her father. He had raised her on all the male testosterone bullshit he had been indoctrinated with in the military. *Figures*, Martin thought. Treat her like a boy, and see what you get. Never easy to get close to. Her mom had died at almost exactly the same age of unexplained causes, so it was most likely genetic, and she had been their first and only child.

Having reached the end of her logic chain, she narrowed her eyes. "If my father so much as *mentions* my condition before I can tell him, I will fly back to Washington and kick your boys so hard you will sing falsetto until Christmas!"

Martin put up his hands. "Duly noted, Bethany Anne, and for the record I'm innocent. I wouldn't abuse your trust like that." Martin didn't even bother with the insubordination. Bethany Anne never meant to hurt friends, but her temper was also apparently genetic, considering the rumors about her father's famous rages.

Cooling down, Bethany Anne strode over to the two chairs in front of Martin's desk and sat in one. She tapped the paper against one of the Christian Louboutins she really enjoyed wearing when working in the office.

Martin could only identify them because of the red soles.

He counted silently in his head, expecting to hit thirty before her next question. He got to seventeen.

It was evident this paper she was tapping on her shoe was orders and she was still gainfully employed. "If you didn't tell the General, and I'm still on the team, why the hell am I being sent out to the middle of the country?"

"That," Martin stated, "is the question of the morning."

CHAPTER TWO

<u>Military Base, Colorado Mountains</u>

"Sir, everything is good. The air inside the vault is now fresh, and the issue with the envelope was nothing, really. The vault must have been hermetically sealed; basically a perfect preservative. Everything in there was exactly how it was when it was sealed." The scientist, one Dr. John Evenich, rattled off the whole thing as if he were giving a lecture.

The General, his sergeant, and a number of techs were down on Level Five.

Reynolds looked at the smaller man and chewed an unlit cigar while thinking this through.

"And exactly when, John, did *that* happen?" the General asked. There were two more scientists going through the room, although there wasn't much to see. It was approximately ten feet wide and fifteen long, with a conference style table in the middle and four chairs—one on each side and the fourth at the far end as if it were the head of the table. There was a knife on a stand in the center, with a phrase engraved on the hilt. No one touched it. Lance couldn't be sure what it said since it was in a different language, but he could guess.

Dr. Evenich looked at his paperwork. "Um, August 24th, 1945."

"So, about two weeks after they dropped the atomic bombs?" General Reynolds continued chewing on his cigar.

"Yes." Dr. Evenich was feeling a little less excited under the scrutiny of the base commander. While not officially his superior —different chain of command—the scientists were here on his "continued good pleasure," which was shorthand for "don't piss him off."

"Well, give me the envelope. I'm going up to my office. It's too hot down here." With that, he gestured to have the envelope pulled off the door.

Dr. Evenich's eyes grew wide. "But General, the significance! We can't just grab it and go. We need to see what is on it; test particulates. It will be scientifically ruined just by our hands touching it!"

General Reynolds' eyes narrowed and he stared at the doctor, still telegraphing his demand for the envelope.

"Dr. Evenich, this says 'To the Base Commander, On His Honor.' Trust me, when someone from 1945 said that, they were *not* thinking about scientists looking at it for clues. I believe this is important. This isn't a democracy, and I'm done discussing the subject. Sergeant, get me that envelope. Men, come out of that room. Leave one guard here to make sure there are no more intrusions. Get those men out, and no one—and I mean *no one*—is to touch that knife until I say it's okay. Am I clear?"

A heady chorus of "Yes, sirs!" rang out.

"John?" The General very pointedly eyed Dr. Evenich until the envelope was brought to him.

Dr. John Evenich, seeing his prized historical object taken away to be pawed by apes after he and others had worked eight months on the base, just shook his head.

Maybe it would be okay to shine a light in there and get some pictures? Dr. Evenich started calling instructions to his people.

. . .

New York City, New York

Carl waited until Michael, the patriarch of the Family, came out of his personal suite inside the massive home. Michael was dressed in a very well-fitting three-piece suit of dark blue with light-gray pinstriping, white shirt, and silver cufflinks. Michael looked to be a young and robust fifty, but Carl knew he was much older physically. He just wasn't sure *how* old. There was barely any gray in his black hair.

It had taken about two hours for Michael to appear from his inner sanctum once Carl had requested his presence. Unlike a normal sleeper, it took a lot to get through Michael's torpor when he was hibernating.

While he was externally calm and collected, one had only to look into Michael's piercing blue eyes to realize the anger that boiled within.

He walked past Carl, who bowed and followed him out of the residence portion of the converted building into the business and operations area. Carl noticed he was just as well built and muscular as he remembered him being five years ago when he had gone into hibernation.

It was as if he hadn't aged a day.

Michael had been expecting to be awakened in five more years. He had checked the date on awakening, and this was too early. He had immediately released his senses to confirm the residence was safe, then checked on his connection to his grandchild here in America.

When he couldn't feel William, he knew the reason for being awoken. Now he wanted answers.

Carl spoke up. "Sir, I've edited a video clip of the operation. It's ready for you to view."

Michael sat down at his desk and woke up his laptop, which was a five-year-old model. Since Michael had no ability to keep up with operating system changes while hibernating, he kept the old operating system until he became accustomed to using the laptop again. At least this wasn't as bad as last time, when he'd had to come to grips with the internet.

He hit the play button on the machine and watched the fifteen minutes of relevant material on how his grandchild had died.

By the end, he had some ideas about what might have happened—not that he could figure out how they had been able to retrieve the serum, or had known what to do with it. Both of those questions needed answering.

However, it did indicate one vital concern. He couldn't just find a good candidate and train them, or have one of his children's children take William's place as he had done for a long time.

No, this time, he needed someone fully trained within the military here in the US. Rejuvenation was also a consideration if he was going to be involved in this campaign.

He would have to request a pre-trained candidate. He had to call on the Debt owed his family.

"Carl, did you start the request through the primary contact?"

"Yes, sir. Frank is still with us, so he's taking care of a lot at that end."

"Good. Confirm my request officially with Frank. I want to know who they're going to send us before I go to the vault. I want to know as much as I can about the three candidates who will be waiting for me."

Here we go, thought Carl.

"Sir, we have a preliminary report from Frank. I'm sorry, but since the last time we implemented the request for Debt of Honor, the military has gotten very good at filtering out potentially unhealthy recruits. The military doesn't want to invest in training, only to find out that investment will die soon."

Carl thought about the requirements for candidates. As he understood them, they were pretty simple. The candidates had to be trained and top twenty-five percent in martial skills, very bright, live with purpose, and (strangely enough for a vampire) very religious. Finally, while the religion requirement tended to cut their options, the last one very nearly did them in.

They had to be expected to die in the next six months.

Washington, DC

Frank was notified that Michael was awake and the Debt was being called in.

Frank sighed. It wasn't that the request was unexpected. In fact, since Bill had been killed, Frank could have won a major bet that this time the requirements were going to be very strict. The last time this had occurred was before any of the current military or spooks had tied their first bootie or put on their first baby shoe.

This was going to ruffle a few feathers. God help them all if someone didn't step up.

Frank *was* old enough—he had been around last time Michael's Debt of Honor was demanded. Most of the military people on the base had lived through that night because one—just one—of those guys had had the honor Michael demanded.

Unfortunately, it had taken two hundred and fifty deaths before anyone figured out Michael was not joking about what was due his family.

More than a few heads had rolled that night.

Military Base, Colorado Mountains

Up in his office, the General was alone with Patricia and the sergeant.

"Kevin, give me some privacy but stay close. Patricia, hold my calls."

Sergeant Kevin McCoullagh waited for Patricia to step

MICHAEL ANDERLE

through the door and then shut it, remaining outside the door at parade rest.

Patricia went to her phone bank and routed the General's calls to her station.

Lance sat down behind his desk and just looked at the envelope for a second. Well, nothing would get accomplished if he just stared at it.

He opened his left topmost drawer and pulled out a metal letter opener with a bald eagle on the handle, its feet clutching the blade. The relic was as old as he was.

When he slid the blade through the crease, it felt like it was a fresh envelope. He opened the letter and started reading.

August 24, 1945

Attn: Current Base Commander

If you are reading this document, then you are in trying times. If you are not aware of any problems, I can state confidently it is due to ignorance.

You will receive a call explaining both this vault and your responsibilities on your Honor (there was that phrase again) *to support the request of Agent Smith (I don't know his real name, nor does anyone else.)*

Be aware that this situation is extremely sensitive, and most information about it was held very close to the vest. In fact, most people won't believe you even should you speak about it.

Lance stopped reading and punched a button on his phone. "Patricia!"

"Yes, General?"

"Call down to Five and tell John and his henchmen they are kicked out. If he gives you any lip, tell Kevin to go down with a few guys and bring them up." With that, he punched off and went back to reading.

Without giving more information than is my right, I will say on my honor that without the help and support of Agent Smith and his Family, we might have failed to catch the actual danger coming from Hiroshima and Nagasaki and selected different cities. There were three agents, not Americans, who went into the cities and brought us proof Japan was creating mutated soldiers and was getting ready to deploy these troops in the war.

In order for there to be no doubt that the base, the soldiers, and the scientists were still inside, these three agents stayed close to the base to verify nothing left before the strike occurred.

They were there when the bombs were dropped.

We owe them so much. We returned so little.

When this vault opens, a charge against our Debt—our honorable Debt—is being made.

On my honor, this day I plead with you to honor our Debt.

Lance read it a second time. *Family* helped us? Lance thought that was strange. Maybe they were from Japan?

He slid the letter back in the envelope and lost himself deep in thought for a few minutes.

His phone's shrilling pulled him out of his thoughts. He yelled at the door, "Patricia, I said hold ALL calls!" Damn, she was getting a little out-of-bounds, not listening to orders. That needed to stop.

The phone switched to speaker mode without Lance touching it.

"General," a deep, gravelly voice intoned, "I assure you Patricia took all the right steps. It took me an extra thirty seconds to bypass her control panel to contact you directly."

"And you are?" asked the General, staring at the phone as if he were deciding whether to shoot it or just beat it senseless. No need to be up this guy's ass until he knew who to give the verbal enema to.

"The man who is going to tell you about the past, the future, and the vault."

New York City, New York

Michael looked up at Carl, who was standing on the other side of his desk. "Carl, are you telling me that throughout *the whole military* there is, and I quote, 'only one' candidate who can fulfill the Debt of Honor?" His blue eyes were piercing.

Michael was very, very touchy about Honor. To him, the word was always capitalized.

"Unfortunately that's the case, sir."

Pursing his lips, Michael asked the follow-up question. "And this candidate is a woman?"

Not knowing where Michael was going with this—he'd never seemed sexist to Carl—he simply agreed. "Yes."

Michael looked down, becoming quiet and reflective for a moment.

Michael could hear Carl's thoughts, and he was right. Michael wasn't sexist in the least. However, Michael, with all his children over the years, had never had a direct daughter.

He had a granddaughter in Europe by the name of Gabrielle, but he'd never met her. She was one of his son Stephen's children…and that child had never created a daughter again.

Not that he'd ever heard negative things about her activities; she'd always produced results. Michael just got the impression the results came with a little baggage.

While that was one consideration, a more significant concern was how often female conversions failed. So far, they'd only had two successful turns in eight centuries—Gabrielle, and one other in Asia. He called that granddaughter "Sunshine" because her full name was too much to deal with.

Many women decided the pain they went through during the transformation was too much to endure. All too often, death was a welcome respite. Better to choose death than become a Nosferatu and be killed when they awoke.

Michael knew this since he had literally written the rule stating they were to be killed.

Michael looked up at Carl again.

"She meets all the candidate requirements?" While Frank was excellent, and Michael didn't doubt his ability, he wanted Carl's thoughts on the matter.

"Yes, sir. Actually, she is a rare achiever. She's top three percent in martial prowess—while she's strong, she isn't a male, and therefore there is a slight deficit. She ranked in the top percentile in intellectual capability on all her tests. She comes from a family where both sides have been military for decades, and her father is presently a general. Her drive is to protect the people."

"Her faith?"

Carl had known the question was coming and was prepared. Finding out about a person's true faith was a little harder, with so many people professing faith but attending their house of worship only once or twice a year. It made it difficult to positively assert any real answer to this question.

"Sir, we were able to get a read on her when she found out she was diagnosed with a strange and rare blood disease. She didn't drop out or ignore her responsibilities after understanding she had little time to live. Her comment was, and I quote, 'all within God's grace and God's design.' The only thing that seems to bother her, as far as we can tell, is not being able to close her cases, and having failed so far to tell her father she's going to die soon."

Michael had looked up from the Bethany Anne Reynolds' dossier while Carl was giving him an overview. "Would she lie?"

Carl hesitated a moment to get his thoughts together.

"No," Carl opined. "I just get the impression she's stoic, like her father. I believe she has a genetic condition inherited from her mother, who died when she was also twenty-eight. Since the doctors give Bethany Anne four to eight months, she might make twenty-nine."

"Our cutoff is six months, Carl." Michael's voice indicated no malleability on the time frame.

"Yes, sir. However, from what Frank has uncovered in the

doctor's report and what's in her official record, it looks like she will live five or six months only if she is very fortunate. More than likely, sir, she has three."

Michael closed the folder. "Well, the quantity of possible candidates is not to my satisfaction. However, these qualifications unquestionably meet the minimum, and in fact, exceed them. Should the military allow the interview to occur, I will consider them to have fulfilled the debt. Should she fail the test, Honor will still be satisfied."

At this statement, Carl was relieved and the tension he was carrying on his shoulders eased. The military could talk about how much ass they kicked all day and all night, and promote honor in commercials. But if they failed in Michael's request, however unprepared they were, they had no idea what they stood to lose for not honoring their Debt of Honor to the Family.

In fact, General Reynolds' whole base might be considered forfeit. Carl hadn't been around the last time this had happened, but had heard about Michael's children taking out "nests" of dishonorable people ranging from hundreds to thousands.

Although this base had probably two, maybe three thousand soldiers and support personnel, this time the patriarch of the Family was awake. Carl was concerned that if the General acted dishonorably, thousands would pay the price for his actions.

Carl knew America had suffered from moral turpitude over the last few decades. Being able to close a deal with a handshake was now possible only in small-town America, for the most part, so Carl was a little concerned.

Fortunately, the military was one of the last governmental organizations which prized honor. While there had been serious issues with honor in the last two wars in the Middle East and in actions against prisoners, Carl hoped General Reynolds represented the older generation—a generation that didn't consider morals to be malleable.

For Michael, the question of a person's Honor was a binary with no middle ground.

It was why both Carl and Frank had been concerned about waking Michael, and why Frank had been so diligent when he ran through the military's personnel databases. He had gone so far as to include the quasi-military groups, such as Bethany Anne's agency, to try to find the best candidates. Frank believed all the candidates had to be perfect both on paper and in person.

While the military argued whether gay people could serve in the trenches, Michael would be opening new opportunities for advancement by the hundreds if this didn't go right.

CHAPTER THREE

Military Base, Colorado Mountains

Bethany Anne drove the rental car, an unpretentious Toyota Camry, to the base entrance and offered her credentials to the guard. After she'd finished her talk with Martin, it had taken her thirty minutes to grab her ready bag and get to the airport and onto the executive jet waiting to take her to Denver. The plane was already scheduled to pick up another person at the Denver airport, so she wasn't able to just land at the base.

While her group had some special responsibilities, her cases had never warranted a private jet. This special treatment was puzzling, and after due consideration, she realized that whatever she was being reassigned to had to be important. This was going to be a very expensive trip for the taxpayers, and regardless of how the media (well, some of the media) portrayed her agency, they were pretty good with their budgets, at least under Martin's leadership.

Taking the credentials offered him, the guard confirmed with the computer that she was Bethany Anne Reynolds and she had business on the base.

It didn't escape his attention that her last name was the same as the General's, nor that she seemed to be spitting mad right now —just like the General, often enough.

Having received her badge back, Bethany Anne thanked the guard and drove to the temporary officers' quarters building.

She still had a few hours before her meeting with the General.

General Lance Reynolds listened raptly to the rough voice on the phone.

General or not, Lance didn't have a high enough security clearance to know a tenth of the total story Frank was telling him. Frank was pretty sure he himself might only know about half of it.

But what the General *did* understand caused him to bite down hard on his cigar, and his irises… Had there been anyone to see them, they'd swear they were going black.

He interrupted his caller. "You're telling me the US military has an honor debt to an independent group of individuals who live inside our borders? Furthermore, that they've been here since before we even became a country, and have been secretly helping us do raids and other black-ops work our best can't handle?"

Frank cleared his throat. "General, if it weren't for this particular Family, we wouldn't even *have* these United States."

The General wasn't sure what he meant by that. "Why? Does this have to do with the two Japanese cities we took out during World War Two? We had another bomb ready to go in about ten days, and we would have flattened the country and made it a glowing parking lot."

A lot of innocents would have died, but that was war.

Frank, used to working with both bureaucrats and officers, continued—because if this General didn't get the message, they *all* were about to have a serious problem.

If the General didn't honor the Debt the US owed Michael's

Family (out of ignorance, Frank felt—not dishonor), things would escalate.

The US military, Frank knew, had one creed that didn't change unless ordered by the President.

The US military never backed down.

Rock, meet hard place.

This would mean Michael's children and grandchildren would start focusing on US military interests, which covered the world. Finally—and this was the kicker—it would mean Michael would wake up any of his immediate children who were still asleep. Many of those children were damn scary.

While Frank couldn't begin to know which side would ultimately win, he knew one thing. America, weak because of its now-decimated military, would be ripe for another country to attack.

"General, let me ask you a question: has it ever, even in the slightest, occurred to you that General Washington was pretty damn lucky?" Frank let the line go silent.

The cigar-chomping stopped. Although the General was loud, he wasn't stupid or slow…and this non sequitur took him only a second to puzzle out.

"You're trying to suggest to me this Family helped win the Revolutionary War?" While a little taken aback, Lance had always known there was something fishy about the history books and some of their explanations of how the battles had been won.

"No, not completely. Obviously, our good men, women, and children took care of most of it. However, there are a few stories that are not included in any of the history books, General, because it would be obvious that we should have had our asses handed to us by the British in a couple of very strategic and important battles. Somehow, against all expected results, we got a win in our column. What I'm telling you is that I have the original archives, and I assure you we would not have pulled out of the dire circumstances. We would have lost, according to all the simulations I've run. General, we had a 96.9% chance of speaking the Queen's English if that Family hadn't been involved."

"So why did they do it? Apparently, they aren't revolutionaries." At least if this contact could be believed, but the whole thing was starting to interest Lance, who enjoyed history.

"That both is and isn't true. They aren't revolutionaries and weren't colonials, but they do fight Evil, sir. And if that didn't come across the line with appropriate emphasis, that is Evil with a capital 'E.'"

"So they came to the colonies to do what, exactly?"

Frank had started to warm to his topic. While he wasn't comfortable being around Michael or his Family, he certainly appreciated what he and the family had done—and still did—for the country.

"This is how I understand it: they had been fighting against certain interests for a significant amount of time before we were a country." Frank hedged his story. Should he admit Michael was the supreme patriarch? No, probably not. If Michael wanted the General to know, he would tell him. He was quite particular about not throwing his role around. "One of the leaders of the Family— they call them patriarchs—was following some pretty nasty characters when they bolted and stowed away on a ship sailing for the colonies.

"He spent a couple of months tracking them down and tying up the business, and when he looked around, he had met and befriended a few of those who were already here. He liked that they were working to build a new society significantly more than he liked the royalty issues plaguing many of the European countries at the time. He sent letters to two of his trusted relatives explaining that he was going to stay to protect this land, and then he disappeared."

"So how did his family get involved with the colonial war?" Lance was very interested now.

"Well, sir, this family member is well educated, very convincing, and extremely wealthy." Frank didn't have to explain how that last part would have been very helpful to the war effort at that time. "Likewise, his family back in Europe, in this case France, had many influential friends at court. He gave Benjamin Franklin a letter to pass to them. Believe it or not, it wasn't all good ol' Benjamin's exquisite tongue that got us the help from the French."

"That's not nearly enough to get them appreciated as much as you're suggesting—"

Frank cut him off. "General, a significant percentage of the funding for the war was supplied by the Family, and it was used to get the necessary materials and favors to help make the revolution successful. Also, the contacts in Europe who shouldn't have gotten involved did. People to this day are trying to figure out how that happened. Finally, there were certain battles that were going to be lost until the patriarch got involved."

Lance heard the singular and wanted clarification. "Just how many of his clan were involved?"

"It's 'Family,' sir, not 'clan.' And there were no others. There was only one of the Family over here at the time. In fact, he himself went into one of the British camps one night...and by the time the sun came up the next morning, not a single man was left alive. This was a fortified encampment, General. This was the larger part of a full battalion; somewhere around eight hundred, I believe. The only people who got shot were hit by random fire from scared men in their own camp. Everyone else had been cut apart by a knife or many knives."

"Where did you research this information? I've never heard that story, and I've studied all the battles of the war." Lance had often wondered about a couple of missing parts, but he'd just figured the victor wrote the history books and hadn't spent the time to research it further.

"Well, let's just say America has a set of history books, and then *another* set of history books. One day, if everything works out, I'll ask you to come to Washington to read some interesting volumes

I have." Frank didn't expect that to happen, but if he could offer the General a carrot, what could it hurt?

"Fine. Assuming I believe you, what now? You said something about the future and the vault?" Lance's eyes were starting to squint again. He could feel a migraine coming on, and he just knew this wasn't going to make him happy.

"Sir, I have a contact coming to see you, who should be there shortly. He's arriving by plane to give you more information. The rest of the explanation has to wait until then for security reasons." Frank was feeling a little better. It at least looked like the General was going to let Carl meet with him. Hopefully, his meeting later today with his daughter didn't derail the whole thing.

"Fine. I'll meet with him at 18:00. Until then, I have a base to run."

"General, I very much appreciate your patience. Thank you." Lance heard the click of the receiver.

He yelled, "Kevin, I need you in here!"

Frank sighed. This would have been so much easier and less stressful if Michael hadn't had to be woken up.

The control tower was quiet. This base, while they had flights in and out, wasn't a major location for Air Force activity, so it could be hours between significant events.

Jimmy Chan, Technician 3rd Grade, was manning the radio when a pilot on the appropriate channel requested permission to land. He was flying a small personal business jet.

"Hold for permission. Stay ten miles out." Jimmy scratched his head. Although the pilot had the protocols, the flight wasn't on the list. He decided to bump this up to the OIC.

"Sir!" he yelled, getting the attention of the officer in charge to come over to his station.

"What do you have, Jimmy?" Technical Sergeant Max Stripten looked at the readouts while Jimmy explained.

"Sir, we have a request to land from a civilian aircraft. They're about eighty miles out, coming in very fast. They were on the right channel and had the right information, but it seems weird we weren't notified."

Max switched Jimmy's display to show incoming aircraft. When he got to the right tab on the screen, it was refreshed, and the aircraft was now shown as arriving in just a few minutes.

"Well, okay, looks like we have them. You're right. That *is* flying pretty damn fast for something that isn't one of ours. I wonder what they have? Hmmm, put them on Runway Three. It looks like they might need the room to slow down. Have them park over by Hangar Five, and let's receive them appropriately." With that, Max stood up. He was walking back to his desk when he got a phone call.

Leaning over his desk, he picked up the phone. "Sergeant Max Stripten speaking." Max laid his pad and pencil on his desk but didn't take a seat just yet.

"Okay, I understand. VIP status, one person coming off the plane, treat as foreign dignitary." Max paused, apparently listening to more information. "Will do, Master Sergeant." Max hung up the phone.

He shouted back to Jimmy, "Call off the special engagement. This flight is apparently VIP. Leave them on three, but switch them over to Hangar One."

Hmmm, Jimmy thought. *I wonder who's so special they get Hangar One?*

Bethany Anne used the keys she had been issued to enter her room, put her suitcase down, and stepped into the adjoining bathroom.

When she stepped out a couple of minutes later, she noticed the yellow message light on the phone blinking.

She rang the desk. "Bethany Anne Reynolds here. I have a message?" She knew she was a little short, but this whole situation just pissed her off.

First, she got pulled off her case, the fucking case she had been closing in on for over four months.

Others? Others had worked on it and gotten nowhere, so she had been handed it as a last-ditch effort before it went into the archives as unsolvable.

Now, she was not only off the case, but she was out of the loop. Who knew what desk jockey they were going to give it to?

She narrowed her eyes. If they gave it to Tim, he would screw it up, and the last thing she would see before she died was the bars in her cell after she choked his ass.

That would be right after she kneed him in the nuts. Since she was going to jail, she might as well get even for all the lurid comments he'd made when no one else could hear him.

The thought caused her to smile a little.

She never bothered with HR for Tim's obvious sexual issues. She figured one of these days she could coax him onto the mat at martial arts practice, and the accidental ass-kicking would be hard to argue. Plus, he wouldn't want to be seen as whining when a girl beat him.

He really *was* a dick.

When the operator spoke, her tinny voice just grated on Bethany Anne's last nerve. "Ma'am, I have a message from the General. He's asked to meet at 18:30 instead of 15:30."

She paused. The operator wasn't sure what else to say. Officer Reynolds was from another part of the service, even if a little clandestine, but she was the General's daughter.

"Fine. I understand, and thank you." With that, Bethany Anne hung up.

Huh, the operator thought. *That went well.*

CHAPTER FOUR

Military Base, Colorado Mountains

Carl listened in on the conversations inside the control tower. *If they only knew!* he thought. *This plane actually is only at sixty percent power.* It really wasn't going all that fast. However, since business planes shouldn't go past the speed of sound, they'd kept it slow.

It wasn't often he used the Family's spying and hacking equipment when not supporting an operation, but if this went bad? Well, then all the rest was going down the drain too. So yeah... he'd decided he was going to make damn sure nobody was getting lazy down there.

Fortunately, Carl thought, Michael hadn't come aboard with him and wasn't at the base.

Yet.

The older gentleman was escorted into the General's office by Sergeant McCoullagh, who supported the man as he sat down. He had to be close to ninety, the sergeant thought.

So far, the General still had little in the way of hard facts about what was going on. He couldn't get through to anyone high enough to give him any insight, and the security clearance of his caller, Frank, had been high enough to indicate someone next to the President.

There were multiple ways to skin a cat, though, and fore-warned was forearmed.

"I appreciate you coming to see me, Mr. Swenson." General Reynolds clasped his hands in front of him, looking at the elderly gentleman across the desk while trying not to show a smile.

Mr. Swenson was thin and reedy. His voice a little breathless, but still strong for his age as he replied, "Hah! Your little fetcher here told me that if I refused his request, you would reinstate me."

The General smiled. "Well, it's within the purview of the US military to make that happen."

Mr. Swenson had been a high-ranking officer in the opera-tions side when he retired. Even though one retired, one could always be called back to active duty.

"Yeah, yeah. I understand you wanted to see me. What's it about, Lance?" Tom went way back with the General. They had known each other when he was getting ready to retire and Lance was just starting his upward movement.

"It's the damnedest thing. I've got a bunch of scientists all over my base looking into dark holes and old boxes, trying to see what went on back in World War Two. I think they hope to find proof of UFO experiments taken from the Nazis or something. Anyway, one of the grunts was down on Five when a klaxon sounded.

"He searched out the noise and found a vault door opening with a note attached about some honor debt we owe somebody. I've had the records checked, and you're the only person who was here during that time who might have a goddamn clue what the hell is going on, so I brought you here to discuss what happened.

"I've got spooks calling me with security clearances that go above the President's and a note from the original base commander who, piss-all, died about seven years ago and didn't leave another note anywhere I can find."

Tom was listening while trying to think back to those days. He had been only twenty when he was here, and his memory was a little spotty that far back. "When was this?"

"A few days after the bombs were dropped." Lance pulled the envelope from beneath a couple of reports he had buried it under.

He tapped it on the desk in front of him, which caught Tom's attention.

"Is that it?"

Lance nodded.

"What's on the other side?" Lance turned the envelope around so Tom could see without handing him the envelope.

Lance was looking right at Tom, so he caught the moment Tom's squinting eyes focused on the phrase, *"On your Honor."*

Those squinting eyes suddenly got very big.

The visitor's plane was taxiing to Hangar One, designated as such because it was the closest to the base's opening into the mountain.

Private First Class Richard Peters drove over to the hangar to 'fetch the dignitary, keep his mouth shut, and be polite.' While waiting for the plane to come off the runway, he got out and walked over to the airmen assigned to help the crew of the incoming plane and struck up a conversation.

"You have any idea who these people are?" He was curious, and he hadn't been told he couldn't ask others.

The airman was obviously chewing some tobacco, and spit to the side before responding in a slow and deep voice, "Naw, ain't got a clue, but it must be some high muckety-muck. Otherwise they'd be in Hangar Two. They usually only open Number One here for the best and the brightest asses to kiss."

As if to punctuate his opinion of the brass, he spat again.

The plane was getting closer. It looked like a really nice Gulf-stream, but something seemed wrong to Richard's eyes and the fellow grunted.

"Well," he murmured, "*that* seems a little diffr'ent."

He clammed up, but Richard just had to know. "*What* seems different?"

"Look at those engines in the back." He jerked his chin toward the plane, which was taking forever now that it was on the ground. "Those aren't standard engines for a civilian plane. Those're military jets on there. I wonder how fast that plane can go? I'd bet my Friday-night poker stash that somebody with some bars and stars had to approve it."

With that, he walked over to show the pilot exactly where he wanted him to park.

Richard assumed parade rest and waited for the plane to stop and the door to open.

Only one guy got off the plane and came down the stairs. He was in a very nice business suit, but he was not typical brass.

Hell, he wasn't even a spook. You could tell those guys when they walked; it was like they were always ready to pounce.

Richard guessed he was just someone with very important business.

Okay, nothing to do but go introduce himself and take him over to the General's office.

———

General Reynolds recognized the look in Tom's eyes. "You remember something, Tom?"

"Yeah, or rather, I remember a story I was told. I wasn't there myself. You say this was down on Five and from some sort of vault?"

Lance agreed. "Yes. The vault looks like it could have come from a bank. No one could open it without serious tools, but for some reason, it opened by itself with a screech we couldn't ignore."

Tom pursed his lips and tried to sit back a little in the chair. At his age, the overstuffed leather seats were damn uncomfortable. Give him a firm chair to sit on, if he wasn't watching TV.

"All right, here's what I remember… I heard the story a couple of months after the Japanese surrendered and things were getting shut down all over the country. We had a few new people come onto the base, which wasn't weird, except all these new guys were going to croak within the next couple of months."

Lance interrupted, "How many is 'a few?'"

"Well, if I remember, there were three. They weren't all from the same service or anything, and they arrived on special flights. One even came in on one of them huge multi-props—special drop-off just for him. *That* got a lot of attention. And then they were all taken over to the infirmary, and a doc checked them. One of the nurses loved to gossip, and we heard it from her. All of them were Special Forces or had seen a lot of combat.

"None of them knew why they had been reassigned here, just that they were going to be interviewed for a position. None of us could figure out why, since they all were going to die soon, so rumor was it was a scientific-type experiment, you know? Something you would be willing to do because, well, you were going to die anyway.

"They were here a few days, and gossip kind of died down and I forgot about it. About two weeks later I ran into one of the techs from the lower levels, and he asked if I had heard the news about the recruits. I hadn't, so he told me they'd been interviewed down on Level Five behind a closed and locked door. They said the three guys went into the vault and the door shut, and about half an hour later it opened again and only one guy came out. The other two weren't inside, and the guy who was left couldn't remember one thing that had gone on in the room.

"Last I heard, he was taken to the infirmary, and they tried to see if they could figure out how two guys could just disappear from a locked and sealed room with ten people outside the door. Not only did he never remember, he died about a week after I was told the story."

"They checked the room for other exits? Never mind, of course, they did."

Lance was sure the migraine was starting to come back. His phone beeped.

Patricia told him, "General, a visitor just arrived. I'm told you're expecting him?" *Damn*, he thought, *I forgot to let her know.*

"Yes. Give me a second to finish with Tom, and send him in when Tom leaves." He let off the intercom button.

"So you think somehow they just disappeared down some science experiment?"

"I don't know. The thing about the last guy...he was really, really interested in his religion after that incident. I always thought it was because he was about to die, and it seemed appropriate. But I talked with one of the MPs who was there when the door opened, and he said the guy just kept muttering, 'I don't have enough faith, I don't have enough faith' and seemed scared shitless, like he had just met the devil."

Lance thought this through for a minute. "So who interviewed him? You said only the three went inside, right?"

"That's right—or at least, that was what I was told. A special plane came in with some sort of civilian at the last minute, but I understand he didn't do the interview. When it was over, he asked the commander to write a letter, probably the one you have there, and close the door. They couldn't open it again, and we just forgot about it after a few months. Most of us were working on shutting down parts of the base."

They talked for a little while longer, but nothing relevant to the mystery or the request came up again. Lance finished by asking Tom a few personal questions, then asked Kevin to take Tom back to his home.

When the sergeant and Tom had left, Patricia came in and introduced him to the civilian who had just arrived from the East Coast.

Just like that spook Frank had said he would.

There was a guard stationed at the foot of the airplane's stairs. It was Michael's airplane.

Carl was unaware, but Michael had been with him the whole trip. He had stayed in his Myst form, so he wasn't visible.

Carl had actually had very little opportunity to find out just what Michael could do. In fact, in Carl's fifteen years with the Family, he had only worked with Michael for about two. Michael had been in hibernation for most of the rest.

Bill had hired Carl at Michael's direction after the Information Specialist position came open. They needed someone who could keep up with all the new computer and internet changes so it wouldn't become such a stressful situation. Their last IS just couldn't keep up.

Michael had directed Bill to install incredibly strong subconscious directions to the previous "eyes and ears" and embedded him a passable cover story before letting him retire very, very wealthy.

He might not ever be able to talk about his past, but he would be able to use his skills and money to create whatever future he wanted.

Bethany Anne was officially annoyed. Again.

She had time, for once, and nothing to do. When you knew your life had a hard stop, you really didn't want to waste any of it.

While she could visit a few areas on the base—and probably

talk her way into a few more if she confirmed her relationship with her father—she didn't play that way.

Her father was a strong man, physically, mentally, and emotionally, but when it came to being a father to a girl, he had never figured it out. Without her mother's influence, Bethany Anne became the little hard-ass one might expect.

If her dad showed his appreciation when she aced studies, she aced studies, and the same when she took up martial arts.

There had been one particular tournament where she knew she wouldn't take first place. Her final opponent was a freak of nature; too massive for any of the moves she could perform to overwhelm him. Any of the obvious ways to take him down would cause too much bodily harm, and he would go to the hospital.

Besides, those moves had been strictly banned at the tournament.

It didn't mean the players didn't try their hardest every other way, but when your opponent had sixty pounds of muscle on you and was damn fast for his size, it got very frustrating.

Bethany Anne was careful to stay out of his range. She was considering how to attack when he started taunting her, trying to get her to strike in anger.

He was successful at getting to her. While she had been taught not to let an opponent's teasing bother her, she had been pretty hot under the collar when she noticed her dad watching her. He had been paying attention, and had apparently understood what her opponent was saying.

Her father realized that in a back-alley fight, her opponent wouldn't have walked away from his daughter.

That didn't sit well with him, she could tell.

When the freak of nature made a comment about her being "a little girl who should just go home," it pissed them both off, and her dad gave her a little sign with his fingers that told her to end it.

She hadn't gone home with a trophy that night. In fact, she had been disqualified. But it hadn't stopped her father from treating her like the new world champion when she left her opponent with an ice bag between his legs, a black eye, a cut lip, and a splitting headache on exiting the floor.

Two others had to help her opponent to walk when he couldn't stand up on his own. She had been banned from the next two tournaments for her rule infractions.

He might not understand how to connect with his daughter at an emotional level, but she knew he was proud of her and would have her back if she ever needed it.

Being a bit prideful, she didn't want to ask.

She decided to go through a few calming exercises before meeting with her father for the first time in over a year.

She didn't know why she was here, but apparently, it was important. She would do what was needed to prepare.

CHAPTER FIVE

Military Base, Colorado Mountains

Carl was introduced to the General and asked to sit in the same leather chair Tom had just been sitting in.

This was Carl's first meeting with General Reynolds, but he had read the dossier Frank had provided—and a few more things he had found that Frank had either failed to locate or had chosen not to pass on.

It didn't matter to Carl. The extra information didn't materially affect his understanding of the General, so Carl placed it in the "overlooked" category.

While Frank had had a lot of information both from inside and outside the government's databases, he still didn't have as much as Carl had access to, so he couldn't give Carl a complete overview of General Reynolds.

General Reynolds started the conversation. "I understand I'm to get information about what's going on from you, so why don't you give me everything from the top?"

Carl sighed inwardly. He knew Frank had already talked to the General; in fact, he had listened in from the plane. He had hoped the General would spare him the overview and allow Carl to fill in the blanks.

It wasn't going to happen that easily.

"General, while I don't have a uniform, I can assure you I work closely with the US government, so I know you've been read in to some degree already—not only to permit me to land and speak with you so urgently but also given some information about what's going on."

"Everything I know," the General exclaimed, "is from a short history lesson a spook in Washington gave me, the rumors a ninety-year-old man I had to drag from his house told me, and the contents of a brief mysterious letter attached to a vault that hasn't seen the light of day in seventy years." He stopped for a moment, looking like he was lost in thought, then continued, "Since it was underground on Level Five, it's a complete mystery. So why don't you try to help me understand why this is such a significant event, and how you pulled enough strings to land at this base and interrupt our assigned mission?"

While Carl was often in the background and rarely in front of others, he wasn't a mouse. Carl had seen enough action, deaths, and close calls that being stonewalled and pushed by a gruff General didn't stress him. Besides, when you worked for the patriarch, General Lance Reynolds' fear factor was a very distant second.

"General, I can tell you more than you want to know. I have knowledge Frank doesn't have, and frankly, I'm not in your chain of command. While I respect your rank, your role, and your authority, I don't have to worry about it. I know, for example, there are things that go bump in the night that scare our best warriors. I work with some of them, General. There are times when our men uncover stuff under rocks, in caves, and occasionally in cities both here and abroad, that would get you committed if you talked about them.

"When our men and women find out about these things, they

go up the chain, and it doesn't take long for Frank to find out about it. He pulls them back, then makes a phone call. That phone call comes to me, General. When your most hardened operatives need help, I am on the President's speed dial. If you need me to, I can pull out my phone and let you speak to the President— because it goes both ways."

Carl stopped, and the General interjected, "You're telling me you're important enough for the President to contact directly? What makes your family important enough for that?"

"General," Carl replied, "it isn't my family, and I'm not *personally* important enough. I'm just one of the important aides, so to speak. Like you, I answer to a higher authority, and *he* is someone who has the respect of the President—and that allows me to call should I need to. It isn't something I take advantage of, I assure you."

Carl felt a coolness in the back of his mind; a presence that had been absent since he left New York.

"So, who is this authority, and what does he want with this base?"

"Sir, we were recently on a mission in Virginia for one of the agencies. Our agent was inside a warehouse tracking three others when they blew themselves up, taking our agent and a full city block along for the ride. It took over a day and a half to contain the fire. While I do not have the authority to demand you never speak about this, I can tell you that if it is determined you have, I suspect you'll have signed your death certificate. Is this understood?"

"No. Why should any of this be top secret?"

"The families are secretive. Very secretive. They've been that way for centuries. The family I work for is not the only one, and let's say that, similar to our geopolitical instability and enemies, the families have been at each other's throats for centuries. It's been relatively quiet for the last seventy years or so, because of what went down in Japan. By the time our agent died, we had enough information for our patriarch to realize the family we bombed in Japan has apparently resurfaced, or at least what they were experimenting on in Japan has."

"You aren't a family member?" The General was trying to figure out how this guy fit into the equation.

"No, I'm what they would refer to as a liaison. Sometimes with the government, sometimes with the grocery boy. On assignments, I have eyes and ears, responsibility, and direct connections to those in the government who are privy to the task. I work with the family agent, or agents, and handle communications and information as needed. That's why I am here right now; to fill you in on this assignment and make sure it goes as smoothly as possible."

"So, what happens next, and what's your role in it?"

"Sir, you should expect the arrival of a candidate for an interview which will happen down on Five. If this candidate passes the interview and accepts the assignment, the duty is permanent, and they will be listed as deceased. Their information will forever be locked away, if not erased."

"*That* black?" In spite of himself, the General was now slightly suspicious and a bit relieved rather than highly annoyed. It didn't seem like he had to do much besides host special VIP Interviews in an old vault and keep it quiet.

"Very much that black, General. This agent will officially die; they will not interact with their old life again. What they become and who they join doesn't exist, so they can't either."

The General took another cigar out of its wrapper and stuck it in his mouth, unlit. "What happens if they fail the interview?"

"They won't remember it. They will come out of the vault and will be checked out medically. Depending on their physical condition, they can either stay or be placed back in active rotation."

The General reached for the envelope on his desk and lifted it for Carl to see. "What about the Debt of Honor?"

"Sir, you write another one yourself and place your new

suggestion on the inside of the vault and close the door. It can only be opened by someone from the Family, and only closed by someone here on the base."

"What happens if we don't allow anyone to be interviewed?" While Lance was slowly coming to understand what was needed, he still didn't like the feeling he was being forced into a situation with precisely one option.

"Would that be 'don't allow,' or 'don't find anybody?'" Carl knew which question the General had really asked, but he knew who the selected agent was. He needed the General to ask the right question and to not only *know*, but to *believe* what the options were.

"I would like the answer to both, actually."

"Well, if there aren't any who fit the criteria and the selection is done by the agency whose representative you spoke with earlier and the Family agrees, then there is no dishonor, and the base commander writes his letter and closes the vault."

"And if we don't allow it?"

Carl visibly sighed, hoping he would be able to convince him.

"Sir, if that happens, the patriarch, or should he not be available, his children, will make sure the person responsible, and all of the men and women he is responsible for, will be considered dishonorable.

"I am not of the Family, sir, so you have to understand I am explaining this as 'what will be,' not that I personally have a say, okay?"

Carl waited for the General's agreement that he understood Carl's qualification. Reynolds squinted at him while he chewed on his cigar, coming to some conclusion before nodding.

"All right, when a person of responsibility is considered dishonorable by a family member, and there is no higher member of the family to request a review, that person and every person who reports to them will be judged dishonorable."

"So, what happens to those considered dishonorable?"

"Death, General. The Family will consider it a bad relationship, and they won't suffer their dishonor."

Clinically detached from the conversation, Carl just had to tell himself, *Wait for it...*

General Reynolds made Carl wait about five seconds before he blew his proverbial stack.

"Are you seriously threatening a General and his entire base? Are you doing this on *MY* base, at *ME*, in my *OFFICE*?" His face was completely red, and two microscopic black eyes of destruction were aimed at Carl.

Okay, Carl thought, *that was impressive. Maybe not to Michael's level, but certainly pretty damned intimidating.*

The General's phone buzzed and Patricia's voice came out of the loudspeaker. "General, is there something wrong? The sergeant is still out here if you need him, sir."

Lance looked down at the phone and stabbed the button with his rock-hard finger. "No, but tell him to stick around." Releasing the button, he looked back at Carl, who stared back. He was composed and ready to let the General cool down...if he would.

Lance worked to get his emotions under control, remembering this wasn't the person threatening his people. He was just the liaison. Lance's real target was his boss.

In a quiet voice, he asked "And just when do I get to talk to the family member? When does he arrive?"

"Sir, he already has."

Michael could tell from his connection with Carl that he had just been introduced to the General and they were about to start talking.

He had been through a lot of the base, and he'd made it down to Level Five by floating through the environmental system. He checked out the vault with the guard outside.

After confirming everything was acceptable and his knife was still present, he went topside again.

While the DNA from the previous three candidates might theoretically be in the hermetically sealed vault from seventy years ago, they wouldn't be able to trace anything to the two who had successfully passed the interview. They already knew about the third one.

He never fully became physically present in the vault when he was in the interview, so *he* didn't leave any evidence.

He continued his exploration of the base. He could discern a difference in the personnel from the last time he was here.

They certainly *felt* different this time. They, as a country, weren't presently under attack, as they had been in the past. The country's efforts weren't as determined, and their purpose wasn't as sharp as that earlier generation's had been. Whether they had wanted a war or not, they had stood up, signed up, and shipped out.

Here and there on the base, he ran into individuals who were going through the motions of their lives. Others were bright, determined, and seemed focused on accomplishing something—although Michael wasn't sure what.

He chose to walk around the base a little. Although he wouldn't be noticed by others, he was posing as a corporal. It allowed him to get a feel for the base flittering around as Myst couldn't provide him.

He chose a building that seemed to house soldiers and walked through the opened door behind two servicemen. He walked past the guard on duty, and another group talking around the front desk.

The passageways were a little narrow, and he had to become Myst a couple of times so others wouldn't bump into his body. Although most people would have just been bewildered, it wasn't worth the small chance that they would talk later and start wondering.

Besides, through Carl's emotions, he could sense the General getting excited. Somewhere ahead he could feel a particularly bright spirit, but possibly it was time to be a little more involved with Carl, or at least more aware of what the General was talking about.

He wouldn't interfere with Carl's job, but he would protect him should the General feel threatened and push back too hard.

Becoming Myst, Michael went as quickly as he could to the General's office. The location hadn't changed since he was here last time.

Bethany Anne slowly finished the calming exercises she practiced often.

Competitive in everything, Bethany Anne realized Death was one adversary who wasn't going to give her a fair break.

She hadn't mentioned it to Martin, but she had seen three more specialists about her condition. None of them could figure out exactly what she had, but it was obvious from her white and red blood cell counts that it was eating her alive.

She had tried a blood transfusion once, and while it had helped, it had only been effective for a couple of weeks. The next blood test came back normal—which meant totally messed up.

The doctors confirmed it wasn't in her bones, or in any of the expected locations where blood cells and blood were either produced or cleaned.

Apparently, a specific defect handed down the generations to her mom had been passed on to her.

Well, *this* genetic disease would die with her.

She wouldn't shed any more tears on what might have been. She had been through that stage already, and while she had needed the emotional relief, she couldn't help others if she was an emotional wreck.

That, she had realized, was her purpose. She had a driving desire to help those who couldn't help themselves. She had no issue ignoring those who *wouldn't* help themselves, and it was a poor day for anyone who tried to take advantage of the system, at least around her. As passionate as she was when someone needed help, she was just as passionate about confronting those who took advantage of the generosity of others.

In her present duty, she was looking into older cases where the people were all dead. It suited her; these people certainly couldn't help themselves, and if she suddenly fell down dead, there wasn't a problem with bringing someone up to speed on the case before it went cold...er.

In her early twenties, Bethany Anne had figured out what drove her: she tried to be the best at anything that would get her father's attention. It took her over a year and four different self-help, healing, and psych books to break the emotional and psychological problems her *raison d'*être was causing in her life. She still enjoyed it when her father was proud of her, but it was no longer something the sun would rise and set on, as those feelings had once been.

Since she wasn't in the same branch of the military and Reynolds wasn't that uncommon a name, she wasn't often identified as being the General's daughter. She didn't shy away from it; she was proud of her father. But she had been brought up to be self-reliant. Wanting to stand on her own two feet was part of the whole package, really.

She looked down at her watch: 18:15. She grabbed her jacket, badge, and purse. Time to meet with the General and find out why he had sent for her.

"Where?" General Reynolds looked down at the composed man in the chair. While Lance was six-ways-to-Sunday pissed, the coldly logical part of his mind recognized Carl wasn't responding to his tirade.

Lance had to give it to the man; he stood his ground.

"That, General, I don't know. However, I can tell you he's been on the base for at least thirty minutes, and since he doesn't drive, I imagine he came aboard the jet with me."

"What, you don't know? That seems unlikely."

"What seems more unlikely? That one person could hide aboard a jet if I wasn't paying attention, maybe in some room—it is a personal jet—or that I've told you that same person may decide the fate of every person in your command?"

"Both. This isn't an either/or question."

"Well, he's a spook's spook. No one I've encountered in either the CIA or FBI feels comfortable around him, and the NSA stopped trying to tail him about thirty years ago, which was before I started working with him. The last time a senior-level bureaucrat became too involved in trying to learn about the families, the bureaucrat was found very dead. Somehow, he had pulled his arm off and then used it to shoot himself six times accidentally. This was inside a very secure location, and trust me...none of the videotapes were of any use."

"What? Did they go static-y, or just not work?"

"No, they worked fine. There was just nothing on them. No one entered or left the building or his office from when he was seen coming back from dinner to when he was found later that night. An aide from a few doors down saw light coming from his office and went to ask him a question. After the investigation, it was learned that the bureaucrat had been trying to find out more about the Family, and had hired a few private investigators with some slush-fund money.

"There were three private investigators. The detectives talked to two, who couldn't remember ever working on the project, but invoices were found where they billed out hours to the politician. The third was located in a psych ward. Apparently, he'd had a total mental meltdown and couldn't even feed himself, much less speak coherently anymore."

"So you're saying this man is running loose on my base right now, and not one of my security people are going to catch him?"

"Sir, I imagine he's going to come into this room, and when he shows up, that door won't open."

"Bullshit."

"No bullshit."

The General stabbed the intercom button on his phone again. "Patricia, have Kevin come in here." He let up on the button.

After a short knock, the sergeant came in. "Sir?"

"Kevin, lock the door and go stand by the window, facing out. Tell me if you see anything or anyone who looks like they might be trying to get into this office."

"Yes, sir." The sergeant locked the door and walked across the office to stand at parade rest, looking outside to see if anyone might be trying to breach the office.

Carl just looked back at the General, nonplussed, and the General squinted back.

"It isn't going to matter, is it?"

Carl just shook his head silently.

The General stared vacantly over Carl's head for a few seconds before suddenly asking.

"How soon?"

Carl's eyes glazed over for a fleeting second. If he had blinked, Lance would have missed it.

Carl stood up and moved beside the chair as if he were waiting for another to take his place.

"General, he's here."

Michael made it to the General's office and was going to Myst under the door when the intercom squawked and heard the

General request that the sergeant come inside. He went in with the man and solidified in a corner, staying outside their realm of awareness. He watched in amusement as the sergeant locked the door and went to stand at the window.

Michael considered the General, looking at his spirit, his demeanor, and how he addressed his subordinate. He could tell from his heartbeat and breathing that he was stressed, but was handling it very well.

He obviously hadn't been a paper-pusher his whole career.

Good.

Michael could see that the General was still quite upset, but was trying to gather enough information to make a decision. He wasn't just going to follow orders blindly.

While that could make this difficult, Michael respected his decisions. He wouldn't agree to order someone to do something he wasn't willing to do himself. Since the General couldn't know what he was going to order someone to do, how could he feel comfortable with it?

However, Michael didn't have too much time, and he needed to get the measure of this man and decide.

Work with him, or start the housecleaning at the top?

Michael moved in front of the General's desk and caught Lance's eyes with his own. It only took a couple of heartbeats to read him.

This man was honorable. Michael would work with him.

"How soon?" the General asked.

Michael spoke to Carl directly, telling him to stand up and move to the side. When he was out of the way, Michael sat down, and when Carl told the General "He's here," he spoke into the sergeant's mind to lock him out and ordered him to continue staring out of the window. Then he materialized in front of the General.

The General's mouth hung open long enough for the cigar to fall into his lap. Good thing it wasn't lit. The General couldn't get his mouth to close for some moments. He suddenly looked down and grabbed the cigar.

Okay, Lance thought, *the suddenly-appearing trick was a little disconcerting.* Lance realized that if the man had wanted to kill him, he would be dead. He wasn't sure about this person or his family having the ability to kill three thousand, but he was positive the headcount would be high. Too high for comfort.

Lance stabbed the cigar he had removed from his lap in Michael's direction. "How the hell did you get in here?" Lance might have been astonished, but this was his office, dammit.

If Lance thought *Carl* was composed, this guy sent Lance's "sixth sense" into serious overdrive. He didn't look threatening in his nice suit and silver cufflinks, but he had just pulled off a spooky trick, and his eyes spoke of age, wisdom...and a complete lack of humor.

And maybe a hint of compassion?

Lance directed, "Kevin, turn around. He's here already." When Kevin didn't turn around, Lance repeated himself louder.

The older man spoke up. "He won't hear you, Lance. When we're finished, he won't remember this meeting even took place."

Lance shifted his gaze from Kevin to the older man and back again. He dropped the cigar on his desk.

Carl told him, "General, we have to leave shortly. However, we will be back tomorrow at 18:00 sharp. I will join you downstairs at the vault. My boss won't be showing up again, and I suggest you don't mention this meeting to anyone except Frank, the gentleman who was on the phone this afternoon."

That seemed like a distant memory at this point.

Lance got his thoughts back in line and glanced at the man in the chair. "Why do you need my men?"

The older man stood up easily and quickly and fixed a cufflink, pausing as if to consider what the General had asked and what he truly wanted to know.

He looked into the General's eyes. "There are battles which you understand. The enemy who stands on a ship, the ones in tanks; some use planes or hit-and-run tactics. They use terrorist attacks, and dishonorably target women and children. These fights you understand; this kind of enemy you can fight.

"How do you fight those you cannot see? Those who suborn the good and command them to do evil? When the protectors need protection, we are the ones who serve.

"We don't give birth to children; we are not blessed that way. We are birthed through unimaginable pain and suffering. One must stand at life's precipice and decide if one would rather sleep forever or become a protector and watch over others as they live their lives."

"The enemy—your enemy—whom you cannot see or defend against has killed one of my family. He sleeps now. I do not have the time to find a qualified candidate from the world and teach them everything they need, so I called in my Debt of Honor owed by your military, who are your country's protectors. From your ranks, I seek to bring another into the Family.

"Will they join? I do not know; that is for them to decide. It is not an easy decision. Either way, Lance, the person would not be with you long. Should they come into the Family, they will protect the innocent from those *you* cannot fight."

Michael continued, "What does a monster look like to those who are good?"

"Like you and me, but with evil intent?"

"What about the monsters themselves?"

"What do *they* fear in the dark of the night?"

"The answer to that, General Reynolds, is *my family*," the supreme patriarch concluded.

With that, Carl stepped back and unlocked the door, and Kevin started to turn around. Lance caught a flicker of motion from the corner of his eye and spun, but the only person Lance saw leave the room was Carl.

The other man was nowhere to be seen.

Carl held the door for Bethany Anne as she came into Patricia's office, then stepped out and closed the door behind him.

Lance motioned for Bethany Anne to wait a minute and quizzed Kevin on what he just witnessed.

Kevin remembered standing guard by the window while the other two talked about something, but he couldn't remember the words exactly. He had turned around when he heard the door unlock.

Lance released him to other duties and told him to have a good night.

Now he had to figure out why his daughter was here. Her agency rarely if ever came to the base in the course of their investigations, and right now was a particularly bad time to have any additional headaches.

CHAPTER SIX

Military Base, Colorado Mountains

Michael could feel the spirit coming his way. This was fire. This was an honorable person. *This was someone he wanted to know.* This was the woman?

While his powers caused everyone to ignore him, he was still physically in the room.

Carl held the door for Bethany Anne as he let himself out. Michael stared at her as she entered the outer office.

She smelled a little different than most humans. Not bad, and although he had read the file and knew the blood inside her was quickly killing her, he could feel its song. What coursed through her veins was as exciting to him as it was unexpected.

Michael stepped out into the corner to watch the woman.

Bethany Anne opened the door to her father's outer office, and a nice-looking man held it for her when he exited.

He looked like he recognized her, but she couldn't remember

ever having met him. Maybe he had seen her in one of her dad's pictures in his office.

Her dad motioned to her to give him a minute through the open inner door and continued talking with someone in his office.

"How are you doing, dear?" Patricia smiled at Bethany Anne from behind her desk as Sergeant Kevin McCoullagh left her dad's office.

She shared small talk with Patricia for a minute, then stepped into her dad's office. He came around the desk and gave her a big hug.

"Good to see you again, Bethany Anne." Lance quickly sized up his daughter. She wasn't happy to be here. Since he hadn't sent for her, he wasn't sure where to go next with this conversation.

"Thank you, sir."

Yup, she was a little frosty. Time to get back into his comfort zone. He sat behind his desk and leaned back in his chair.

"Take a seat, and tell me why you're here. We don't normally see anyone from your group at this base."

She sat in the same chair the older guy had just vacated, reached into her purse, and pulled out a folded piece of paper.

"I'm here because I was directed to meet with you today at 15:30. I figured something had happened and strings were pulled. I was yanked off my case, stuffed in a jet and sent here first class. I assumed you were behind it." Bethany Anne didn't relax her posture as she perched on the edge of the chair.

Lance reached for the orders. "I didn't order you to come here, Bethany Anne. In fact, the timing is pretty bad. Let's see what your orders are, and if I can, I'll send you back...after we have dinner together tonight."

Her father had never lied to her. Didn't he know anything about her orders? This was either getting stranger by the minute, or there had been a colossal screwup in paperwork somewhere. She handed the orders to her dad. "I thought you had to know about it. All it says is to come to the base and present myself to you, and I would learn more from a letter titled 'Our Debt of Honor.'" She looked at the General.

Bethany Anne had realized her father hadn't been giving this meeting his full attention. She had enough experience growing up with him to recognize when her father was mentally elsewhere.

But when she finished speaking, his expression changed to a look she wasn't used to seeing.

His face went totally white. Ashen. He looked afraid. The only other time she'd seen this look was when her mom died.

He opened the letter and quickly glanced at the contents. There wasn't much there. It wasn't as if her father could misinterpret anything, so she wasn't sure why he kept staring at it.

Lance took the letter from Bethany Anne, but he had a hard time concentrating. His heart wanted to beat too loudly right now.

This couldn't be right.

He felt hollow. If *Bethany Anne* was the interview, he was going to lose her—just like her mother Meredith.

Lance had always had a lump of bitterness and anger inside his heart. He knew he had in some way been responsible for killing his wife. She had been too young. He had believed since she died that if he had focused on her more, he could have seen something early enough to get help. Somehow there had to have been a cure for whatever had killed his wife. Medicine had advanced, so there should have been something they could have done.

But no, he had focused on his job. His career. He felt comfortable there. He loved his wife, and her smile never failed to bring a smile to his face, but he had been promoted quickly with the military. He assumed he had plenty of time later to settle down and enjoy his personal life.

He wasn't going to wait until retirement, he had promised

himself.

Their daughter had been born when Meredith was twenty-four and he was twenty-six. Meredith gave Bethany Anne so much attention that he felt justified in focusing fully on his job.

He never saw the signs that she was sicker than maybe a cold or the flu until one Sunday morning when he rolled over and she was gone. Oh, her body was there, but her soul had left during the night. He hadn't noticed that happening, either.

Bethany Anne had been too young to understand, but he had sought help for himself. He was able to work through part of the grieving process, but when it came time to forgive himself, he took the crushing blame and packed it into his heart.

For what he had done, he deserved to repent for the rest of his life...and he was going to. It didn't matter what the psychologist had told him.

But as he stared down at the paper in his hands, he thought maybe his penance hadn't been enough. Lance might not have been a perfect father, but he had tried to make up for his mistakes. He cared deeply for his daughter and had brought her up the only way he knew how. He had made sure she could stand on her own two feet both intellectually and physically. Bethany Anne had gone to a very expensive private school and graduated summa cum laude.

She had been chased—some might say harassed—by the best universities in the nation. Major corporations had also pursued her with their checkbooks open, but all she asked for was a chance to serve.

The CIA had grabbed her in a second, only to lose her in two years after her basic courses were finished when she went into the black agency hole of no return. Even *he* didn't have the security clearance to know everything that went on in her group since the agency's mission was so dark. He had been happy she had wanted to serve, but he had known she would be wasted in his branch.

While he had felt the CIA would be a little stressful for *him*, *she* would do fine. When he found out she had been recruited for other duties, which had pissed off her CIA bosses, he was careful not to let her see it concerned him that she might go into black ops. While she was certainly mentally and physically fit enough, he didn't think she had that certain *something* spooks and black ops operatives had to enable them to do the dirtier deeds.

When she had told him she had been put on research projects and cold cases, he had been relieved, but he had heard the disappointment in her voice. He knew she wanted something in the action.

He had just told her she apparently needed a little seasoning.

When she had closed a couple of major and politically sensitive cases, one involving a spy deep in their agency and another with a high-ranking senator, she had seemed pleased with her role. He hadn't heard her talk about wanting more action-oriented roles for a while.

He knew that her boss, Martin, was incredibly pleased with his recruit. Lance didn't bend any rules, but he had checked up on her surreptitiously a couple of times. General or not, she would come down on him like a ton of bricks if she thought he was helping her out in any way. She stood on her own two feet and made things happen because of who *she* was, not who *he* was.

Just like he had taught her.

So he had never made any special calls on her behalf...ever.

But now? Now he wanted to in the worst way possible. He wanted to stab the intercom button and tell Patricia to get that spook in Washington on the phone to tell him to shove offering *his daughter* as an honor sacrifice up his ass.

Spook or not, Carl's boss could have his daughter when he pried Lance's arms from around her shoulders. He had lost his wife because he hadn't been there for her when she was sick. He wouldn't fail his daughter.

But now he had to face something he had feared as Bethany Anne grew older.

His daughter was going to die.

Michael had changed to Myst and followed Carl out of the office. He had watched Bethany Anne talk with Patricia, and studied her.

With an internal sigh, he sent Carl a message to go back to the plane; he would meet him there later.

The plane had everything they would need to stay the night. There were only two of them, and Michael didn't need much room to sleep. In fact, there were only two ways to access the area where he slept, and both were so small you couldn't fit a hand into them. The pipes, after a couple of twists and turns, opened into a small area underneath the bedroom in the back of the plane. It was part of the bedroom, but there was a metal plate between his section and the bed above. While he couldn't Myst into the area from outside the plane normally, he could open a small hole for his entrance and exit while the plane was on the ground. If he left the plane and failed to get back on before it took off, it would automatically close before the plane hit a hundred miles per hour...and he would have to return to wherever he needed to be some other way.

He'd had the modifications done after he took possession, and none of them were shown on the plane's schematics. Those who had done the upgrades had had their memories changed; they couldn't remember doing anything but a few touch-ups to the interior bedroom in the back.

That was where Carl or William would have normally slept.

Michael was a sunwalker, as was one other of his children, but the sun would destroy a grandchild; It would take only minutes before death by exposure. By the third generation, death would be instantaneous. Something had mutated—weakened—in the blood that had been passed to succeeding generations.

Most of them could stay awake during the day, but they

weren't superhuman; they needed sleep like anyone else. Since most were affected by sunlight, it was just more convenient to sleep during the day.

For vampires, blood was useful, but it wasn't quite a "drink or die" situation. It was the ability to exercise other talents that required the energy blood afforded every vampire. Those whom they fought, the Forsaken, harvested humans and drank at least weekly. The more they drank, the more their changed bodies craved it until it was all-consuming for them. They were the true vampires of old; the evil monsters the tales were told about.

Michael had been fighting Forsaken and Nosferatu for so long that he was tired and slept often. His body aged about one year in ten when he was awake, and perhaps one year in twenty when he slept.

The belief that vampires were forever young was inaccurate. If you considered how much a normal person would age in fifty years; a vampire would only look five years older. If he had slept, then the vampire might only have aged a couple of years.

There *was* one way for a vampire to roll back the time on their body: they could create a new vampire. When the process was finished, their body would become about the same age as the new acolyte.

This was not a problem for those his family fought. They had no concerns for those they turned, or whether they died. If they changed someone who died during the process, they would shrug and walk away years or decades younger, leaving a dried-up husk behind.

Just another missing person case.

Michael had only turned six in his life to date, and none since he had come to America.

He hadn't had a sire. His change had been unique, and certainly more painful than most he had been privy to.

His human existence had come to a pretty early end in the mountains of what is now called Romania. The alien essence which had created vampires sought to ride a human's body, changing it to something more like its original host—or so he believed. Michael had never figured out if his...benefactor...was from this universe, or elsewhere.

The virus was part of him. If he drained a human and exchanged blood to turn the person, his blood overcame the host's ability to protect themselves. Michael believed it was at this time the challenge to a person's soul occurred.

The first stage brought agonizing pain throughout the nervous system. The body wasn't physically hurt, but every nerve felt like it was on fire; rough and raw. It was as if the body had been dropped into a pool of acid and was being eaten from inside as well as outside. A lot of humans just died at this point. Why keep living when you had no idea how long the pain would last?

Michael had seen some of the strongest give up at this stage... and some of the most physically frail persevere.

The human's thinking brain was offline; all it could do was feel the pain.

Slowly a person regained the ability to think through this pain, and it was at this stage the most insidious attack occurred.

The virus would tempt the host. Once the change had begun, the host had already mutated enough that the virus would continue to live, and it would seek blood with an unquenchable desire. Here the virus would whisper into the host's mind that they had become gods. How, if they would just allow the virus to take control for a little while, it could stop the pain that was causing them to scream and gnash their teeth, and give them rest.

Oh, but the lie it told. If the host agreed, the virus would lock out the host's will. The person would be a passenger in their own mind while the virus became a monster of legend, listening only to the desire for blood or the commands of their maker.

These would become Nosferatu, with no humanity left. Possessed of incredible strength, cadaverous gray skin, and red eyes, the host would rise to kill and drink anyone or anything they could hear, see, or sense. It would go on a killing frenzy until it was satiated, then it would find a place to hide while it finished the transformation safely. When the host finally awoke, the original soul was no longer in possession…and would never be again.

With each successive generation, the virus became weaker, and the challenges to overcome were less. This helped some make it through the transformation with their soul intact, but that vampire's power and abilities were never as great as its parent's. If a host were to overcome the virus and then fall into mental exhaustion, they would lose their memories and possibly their knowledge and wake up as but children. They would need to be taught all over again how to eat, how to walk, and how to talk.

Those who were barely able to overcome the virus would be weak as vampires—still stronger than most humans, but certainly more useful in supporting roles which didn't require them to think. They followed orders very well.

The longer the host fought the virus, the more of themselves they retained. Should they fight all the way through until they woke up, the new vampire would be as strong as their potential allowed, and would remember everything before their transformation.

Even with the careful selection Michael required of any of his family, to have a candidate make it all the way through the conversion was still an unusual event.

So, he required any in his family to select only from those who were going to die. If the selected were to choose death over the pain, then at most they would lose six months of their life. If the virus were able to persuade them to allow it to take control, then when it opened its red eyes, it would be decapitated before it blinked.

Michael's family *never* allowed a Nosferatu to live. Those were what they fought, and had been fighting for ages.

There were two groups of combatants in the vampires' struggle: Michael's Family—and everyone else.

CHAPTER SEVEN

<u>Military Base, Colorado Mountains</u>

Bethany Anne could see many emotions crossing her dad's face. It was rare he didn't keep a shield up, so she knew he was hurting.

It had been a long time, but she let her professional demeanor relax and set aside the mask of toughness she wore while out in the world.

"Dad, what is it?" She reached across the desk and took one of his big calloused hands.

He looked into her eyes. "How long do you have?"

She stared at him, blank-faced for a minute while her mind raced. It was obvious he hadn't known when she got here that she was sick. If he had, he wouldn't have just hugged her and gotten straight down to business. In fact, until he read the orders, he hadn't really been thinking much about her being here.

So what had changed? Why had her orders upset him so much, and tipped him off to ask her about her medical issue? And should she answer the question? Lying was out. He didn't lie to her, and she wouldn't lie to him.

She might, however, not answer the question.

MICHAEL ANDERLE

Her indecision was reflected in her eyes.

He asked her again softly, "How long?"

She sighed. "Six months. The doctors could be wrong. They don't understand how my blood cells are so messed up, but they can't find any problems with me. I've been to four specialists so far."

Lance straightened a little in his chair, and his eyes lost their unfocused look. "Then I guess we'll go to a fifth, and a sixth. If we have to see another ten doctors, Bethany Anne, we will do so. I won't let this take you."

"Dad, I've worked with some of the best. I asked Martin for a couple of favors, and he was able to get me in to see some highly placed specialists—"

"Martin knew about this and didn't tell me?" Lance's face started to gain color again since he had a target to focus on.

Bethany Anne stopped that cold.

"He had no right to tell you! It was my decision, and I asked for his promise to tell no one. If I hadn't needed him to make the requests for me, I wouldn't have told him, either. This is *my* fight, *my* battle, and I *will* make it happen my way."

She stood up and started pacing in front of his desk, causing his head to swivel like he was watching a tennis match.

"I am my own person, Dad. I have a right to live my life however I want to. By the same token, I have the right to decide how I'm going to die. I've worked through my grief. While it may come as a shock to you right now, I carefully considered what happened with Mom, and I think at some level she knew something was wrong. She made her decision to do as much for me as she could before she died. You always said she was with me morning, noon, and night, and now I understand why. I don't have children, and I'm thankful for that. However, I want to help those who can't help themselves, and if that means working my cases until I don't wake up one morning, then that's how it's going to happen. I'm not going to run from one doctor's office to the next and one lab to the next, having so much blood taken I can't even get out of bed. That's not the life I want to live, and I won't go down that path. You told me Mom was never bedridden, right?" She stopped pacing to stare at him.

He had so many emotions going through him. Could she be right? Could Meredith have known? Why wouldn't she have told him? "That's right."

Bethany Anne picked up a rock paperweight from his desk. She had given it to him on her sixteenth birthday and told him it represented the rock he was in her life.

"So I might as well continue working until the day God takes me home. If I can help one more person, it beats waiting on Death." She put the rock down and took a seat.

"How do you know everything has been tried? I know we could have found something to help Mom if she would have just confided in me. I wasn't the man your mother needed, but I won't let *you* go." Lance's eyes were hooded by memories and pain.

He was feeling the pain of the past. She had seen him do this from time to time. "Dad, you've never let me go. You raised a hell of a woman, one I am proud to be. You allowed me the opportunity to become who I am. Whether I have ninety years or just twenty-nine, I'm proud of my life. There are many who make it to seventy and can't say that much. I can. I'm sorry I waited this long to tell you, but I couldn't face hurting you, I didn't want to see the pain in your eyes, or bring you the pain I see in your heart right now. I'm sorry, I'm not proud of how weakly I've acted in this. I wanted to live my life my way, and if I didn't have to talk to you right now, I'd have just kept on until close to the end."

She leaned back in the chair. She had said her piece the best she could. No parent should go through the death of a child…and she'd had to be the one to tell him. If she could have run away from this, the temptation might have been too much.

She spied the orders, still sitting on his desk. She wanted to know what they meant, and how they affected her. Like she had thought before, she'd had a hard stop, and time was wasting. Maybe this could get her dad to come up for air.

"What are your orders, General?"

Lance looked up and followed Bethany Anne's eyes to the forgotten orders she had handed him.

Orders? he thought. His orders were for her to see more doctors. His orders were for her to not accept this result. His orders were to, well...to live.

And, to a point, Lance realized she *was* living. She hadn't allowed this death sentence to stop her from doing that. She was living what time she had left her way, on her terms—just like Meredith had. Meredith hadn't lost faith in him. Meredith had had total faith he would carry on like the soldier she knew him to be.

A tear formed in his eye. His wife had had total faith in him and had spent every minute she could with their daughter. *She* had been the rock his family was built on, not him. Now his daughter was the rock, and he was just figuring this out. Why was it that people never saw the obvious?

The older man's voice came back to his thoughts. *"We are the ones who protect the protectors. We are the ones nightmares fear."* Tom's comment that maybe they were doing scientific experiments on those who were going to die soon came to mind as well.

They all knew it. Carl, the spook in Washington, and the older man. They had all known Bethany Anne was the person who would be interviewed. Frank had tried to tell him the Family worked for the protection of people. Carl had told him the operative would officially die in the records—just like Bethany Anne was going to die in just a few months.

Finally, the man had told him his family wasn't created like a normal family. That they recruited those in the military and others. They searched for very special, very unique people—and they had now requested Bethany Anne. They wouldn't have done that if they thought she was just going to die in a few months.

They knew how to fix this blood issue, but they weren't saying so. He felt a little hope, but how to reconcile that he would never know what had happened?

He tried to gather his thoughts about everything that had gone on that day. His intuition guided his decision. He didn't know all the answers, but he did believe one truth: Bethany Anne's best chances were with her orders.

He might not ever try to find out about *the* family, but if Bethany Anne disappeared tomorrow night in that vault, he sure as hell would continue to search for *his* family. If that pissed off Carl's boss, well, he could just come talk to him about it. It wasn't like he would be hiding.

Carl nodded to the soldier on guard duty outside the plane and climbed into the aircraft. They had connected power so the engines didn't have to run. He went ahead and hit the button to close the ramp after letting the guard know to be careful when it came up.

He wasn't sure how Michael had gotten to the base. He had not felt him during the trip, and he hadn't been aware of him boarding the plane ahead of him. While he hadn't gone back into the rear bedroom to see if anyone was in there, he was pretty sure the pilot would have mentioned something about it when he got on the plane.

If Michael needed Carl to open the door for him, he would certainly know about it.

Carl went over to the bar and poured a small amount of Drambuie into a glass. He didn't like it on the rocks; it just watered down the liquor. Carl had never actually been drunk, but he did enjoy a small amount after an operation—and right now he was wound up tightly enough to feel like he had been on an operation.

He sat back in one of the luxuriously upholstered seats. There were only six in this plane, plus the bedroom. You could sleep in any of the seats since they all laid back, and there was a small kitchenette and bathroom up front. They were good for a few days of living on the plane.

Michael typically didn't interact much with anyone when he was awake. When Bill was working, you could toss a coin sometimes to figure out if he would talk with the humans around him. Carl had studied him for a while and realized that if it was a new group, he probably would speak. If they worked with that group for the next few years, he would keep talking. It was only after about five to seven years that he would stop fraternizing with them.

In Carl's fifteen years with the group, Bill had looked to be in his mid-thirties. He had died looking the same age.

Carl had talked with Michael about what he had seen on the videos. Michael had explained Bill should have remembered the stories about how the three agents had died in Japan so many years ago.

Bill wasn't one of Michael's sons. He was a grandchild, but he was still incredibly powerful. He had lasted a long time during the transformation, as Carl understood it; somehow persevering during the transformation affected their strength.

Bill was a bit of a ball-buster, but he had been fun at times, too.

Carl wasn't a complete nerd. He enjoyed watching most sports, and an occasional MMA fight. He loved Indian food, but the spices drove Bill's hypersensitive nose up the wall.

He wouldn't overindulge too often, just frequently enough to poke the lion and make life interesting.

He had made sure never to call him "Billy Boy" or anything like that—except while he was on a mission and couldn't immediately retaliate. Bill had been an easygoing vampire, all things considered, and if Carl didn't piss him off after the mission, he would usually just let it go.

Carl was going to miss him.

He was getting to the bottom of his drink.

He wasn't sure when Michael would get back, or if he would come on board. Carl had realized early on that sunlight didn't affect Michael like it did Bill. That alone showed Carl how different they were.

A couple of times Carl had been allowed to watch them spar in the basement.

If he could have *seen* the fight, he was sure it would have been spectacular. But he had heard and felt it more than seen it. Michael would come down dressed in his black gi, Bill in his yellow gi. After some discussion, Michael would show Bill how to attack or block a move, and then let Bill throw him for practice. All this took place at a natural human pace—and then they would get serious.

It just looked like a bunch of fast movements until you heard Bill's body hit the mats. Michael would explain what he had just done to Bill, and let Bill try it at human speed. Then they would fight until Bill was on his back again.

Carl thought Bill fighting Michael was about on par with the couple of times Carl tried to take on Bill—which was to say, impossible.

For a human who wasn't special ops, Carl was very good at fighting and with weapons. Well, he was good with guns. He totally sucked at other martial weapons. While he understood and was able to handle hand-to-hand combat, for the most part, he just didn't like edged weapons.

He studied them. Often as the eyes and ears, he'd had to be able to describe and name all sorts of weapons, whether they shot projectiles or had been crafted hundreds of years ago.

Considering some of the jobs they had worked on, Carl was happy to be safely out of the danger zone.

His mind mellowed and relaxed. It had been a very tense few days since Bill had died and Michael had been awakened. This was the first time he wasn't focused on getting through the interview without scores of people dying and a price on his head.

He didn't think the military would only blame Michael for everyone's death. Somehow Carl thought "aiding and abetting" would be attached to his name, and he would go down as well.

Ride the tiger, and sometimes it will turn and bite you.

They had handled some incredibly important ops—not just for the nation, but occasionally the world—and they were as black as ops got. There was never any proof of what had happened. If there had been, he wouldn't have been doing his job very well.

Carl snorted. That was something. If he did his job perfectly, there wouldn't be any proof he had done his job.

He wasn't the best hacker in the world, but with the equipment and contacts the family had, he was certainly in the top one hundred; probably top twenty. Half the others in the top twenty belonged to major countries, either in their spy or military services, six worked for corporations, and one worked for the American Council of Weres. Of the other three, two were in the black market, and one was in Michael's family, over in Asia somewhere.

So, how had someone found out where Bill and I were going to hit, anyway? Carl wondered. He put down the glass, now empty, and pulled out his laptop. This aircraft had its own connection to the internet, which randomly made requests to Netflix and had a couple of background applications running fake research requests. Underneath this traffic were the real requests. Carl got busy tracking down information on their enemies.

All this was being done inside the video streaming in the network traffic. Carl didn't believe for a second the military wouldn't intercept and try to sniff any and all packets to see what was going on with their communications. They were sitting on a government base, for fuck's sake. If Carl had been the other guy, *he* sure as hell would be stealing all the info he possibly could.

One of the best ways to annoy those who tried to decrypt your data was to provide a data line with high-level encryption you knew would be decrypted after a significant effort—and have the data inside that stream be complete gibberish. The packets looked like another encrypted communication, so the opposing team focused on the obvious. If your video packets looked and worked well, they wouldn't make the effort to see if you were sneaking anything else in.

All this for $9.99 a month. Thank you, Netflix.

That attitude was what had gotten Bill's attention fifteen years ago, and it was a good attitude to have today.

Carl couldn't bring Bill back, and he most likely couldn't hurt whoever took him down.

But if he could find them, Michael would certainly want a word with them.

CHAPTER EIGHT

<u>Washington, DC</u>

Frank worked in the basement deep under an older building in Washington, DC. He was near a couple of underground pathways, which were very useful when he needed to meet with vampires who couldn't take the sun.

His arthritis acted up during the winter since it got quite cold down there.

He was too damn old for this, and he knew it. It was time to bring in someone else to take control.

He could and did tell himself he had stayed out of patriotism, but he really couldn't lie to himself. He hadn't left because he enjoyed the game too much.

When he was tapped to take over from his predecessor, Frank had known a few people in and around the city. He had been on the staff as a naval liaison during the war.

Young, but not dumb, and with his family connections, he was known well enough in the right circles.

He had been approached in the middle of the war and recruited into this section. Having had it explained that what they did was top secret, Frank couldn't wait to get into the action.

He often wondered if he would have been more hesitant if the war hadn't been going on at the time.

He had wanted to be in on the action and didn't understand that helping his Navy boss was helping take care of the Nazis.

By the time he had understood he wouldn't be on the front line, he was in too deep to back out without needing part of his brain yanked out of his head.

There were secrets the military and government kept from their people for good reason: it allowed them to sleep at night. It was the responsibility of the few who knew about the nightmares to shoulder the burden for the rest of the nation.

Many felt the President had it worst of all. A few who knew the secrets would occasionally argue amongst themselves over brandy and cigars when they were alone together.

Everyone had witnessed how those who accepted the presidency went into the job looking young, only to have aged beyond their years by the time they stepped down.

It wore on a person. The weight and shouldering of responsibility usually did.

Frank would normally have left his position a couple of decades back, had Michael not given him a light rejuvenation. He had never understood how it happened, exactly. It had been back in the 1990s, and they'd had a nasty little underground war going on in South America that was backed by one of the Forsaken families. Michael had come to visit him one night when he was working late, trying to pull information from the government's assets down in Brazil.

They'd had a good talk about what he wanted to do, and what kind of person he believed he needed to find in order to be comfortable about passing the baton.

He remembered admitting he wasn't happy having to give up his post. He liked doing the job. He might not have ever been on the front line, but like Carl, he understood that he really wasn't the right person for the front line. For one thing, he wasn't dead yet.

Not that vampires were physiologically dead. They were humans who had been transformed into...something else.

When he had just started with the group, he hadn't listened to his mentor and had tried to find out more about the Family. Fortunately, his mentor had been watching for him to do just that and had stopped it before any of the requests had filtered through the security net.

He had come in one morning to find his mentor waiting for him with a sheet of innocuous-looking questions that Frank had carefully worded so as not to raise any suspicions. His stomach had about dropped out of his body when he realized they were his.

He had passed a test, somehow, with those questions. He'd been hired to take over the role, and to perform, he had to be smart. His office only had one top-secret-level dispatch line. He hadn't known at the time that it went straight to his boss, who would then either approve his request or hold it.

He had held onto all of Frank's requests for information for a week to collect them. When Frank hadn't requested any more info for two days, he'd come into the office and had the talk with him.

Apparently, his boss had done something similar, and his boss's mentor had been prepared, just as Frank's boss had been prepared for Frank's attempt. When the time was right, he would do the same for his protégé. If his protégé didn't try this, they weren't the right person for the job. They would wake up in a hospital with a mild form of amnesia. They would probably only forget two or three months.

His boss/mentor shared some of what he knew after he was able to convince Frank that to have released the cables could have had potentially dire consequences, not only for himself, but also the agency and the military, and would have given the enemy a huge boost.

Should enough people find out what was going on, then Michael's family would all eventually be found and killed. With their ethics, they wouldn't be able to grow their family faster than they could be destroyed, for sure. The enemy did not subscribe to the same ethics as Michael did. Oh, they could certainly be hurt, but they didn't care if a person wanted to become a vampire. Their family could grow so much faster in times of need, without the worry over moral issues.

For the enemy, growth was always a balance between a need for new members and the potential that a new member would eventually challenge the leaders for supremacy. In their families, it was about survival of the fittest, and one way to survive was to limit how many potential challengers there could ever be.

If they didn't have children, those children wouldn't commit patricide.

His mind had always been agile. Even now, he didn't feel like he had lost any of his keen intellect.

Unlike others, Frank knew keeping physically active helped the mind to stay sharp, so much more than those silly games on everyone's smartphones and online. He should know; he had access to the latest research, whether it had been published or not.

When he had spoken to Michael two decades before, he didn't remember finishing the conversation. He had woken up on the couch that doubled as a bed when he needed one—and had received the shock of his life when he looked in the mirror in the office suite's bathroom that morning to shave.

He appeared twenty-five years younger; instead of being in his mid-sixties, it was like he had just turned forty.

He knew Michael had done something to him but didn't know how it worked. For whatever reason, Michael had seen fit to extend his usefulness.

He still felt—and was—fitter than he should be in his late nineties, but he knew there wouldn't be an extension this time. He had not lost any of his desire to be in on the action, but it was time for it to be another generation's game. With changes in the world came new attitudes, and Frank's attitude, he noticed, wasn't very adjustable or easygoing anymore. He needed to be able to work with those he contacted, and to accomplish that required empathy. Frank realized his ability to be empathetic had diminished over the years. Too many times he'd wanted to just use a two-ton hammer to get through to the bureaucracy he found himself having to deal with when the military and local first responders kept asking questions. In his generation, if someone obviously way above you spoke, you listened and obeyed orders.

Now he had to deal with people trying to figure out what was going on *much* too often. The internet was both a great help and a huge problem for his group. They were able to find out about new outbreaks and problems quickly, and there were those who would get together in chat rooms and create wiki sites, comparing their research to ascertain what was going on.

Most times, it wasn't anything to worry about. Other times, he would see if those who were doing the work had anything in their backgrounds to warrant a mention to the local police or tax office that might give them reasons to focus on other things in their lives.

He had found out one particular troublemaker was a bit of a Casanova, having three girlfriends who knew nothing about each other. Frank was kind enough to send two of them a request to meet at the romantic restaurant where the guy was on a date with the third. Frank hadn't realized exactly how nasty it might become; the lady who was at the table with him had taken her steak knife to the guy.

When Frank found curious people who had nothing for him to use as leverage, he would pass the information to the liaison—and within a few weeks, that person would find something else that fascinated them, and they would drop off the supernatural interests group.

He had been quietly researching for the past two years to

narrow down his list of potential recruits and had identified a handful he considered promising. Bethany Anne Reynolds had been his top choice—until he had learned two months before that she was going to pass away.

He had researched her exhaustively as his successor for over a year. There had never been a female in his job, and he wanted to make sure the first one to work with the group made the right impression with Michael. He hadn't expected Bethany Anne to end up on the short list to be transformed.

Over the months of researching and watching her, he had grown to like this determined young woman. He had already mentally tagged her as his replacement and felt a responsibility, as if she were his star pick to become the football team's next quarterback.

She needed good backup. Carl was becoming a good liaison for Michael's team, but with Michael awake and probably not going back to sleep soon, she would be learning from the patriarch himself.

Everyone was going to need to step up their game, and Frank was worried he had little game left to offer.

He had four other possibilities. He needed an update on their activities, and to find out if any new agents might be available.

Military Base, Colorado Mountains

Bethany Anne watched her father's face go through different emotions as she waited for the orders to be explained to her. She wasn't sure if he would try to order her to seek more treatment, but if he did, she would have to push back regretfully.

She was fairly confident her assignment didn't have anything to do with trying to get her healed, so she could strike that down. However, in some form or fashion, her orders had given him insight into her condition he hadn't had before she'd walked in.

Therefore, he must have been expecting someone suffering from a fatal disease to show up.

The clues she had put together since arriving suggested something was happening that wasn't a straight-up military project. That was her working hypothesis.

So what special request would require someone of her talents and skills—and mortality status?

She pondered this while her father was concentrating. As Martin had expressed to her before she left, "That is the question."

She just didn't have enough information to form a solid answer.

"Bethany Anne," His voice was a little gruff from emotion, but he had it under control. "I'm not positive about everything I'm about to tell you. I can explain that to the best of my understanding this is top secret, so you and I are held to the strictest confidence."

He waited until she dipped her head in acknowledgment.

He told her the story, starting with a klaxon sounding on Level Five and ending when she had walked into his office.

It took only a short time for Michael to form an opinion of this lady. If Bethany Anne and the General met him tomorrow night, he would accept her. The door to the vault would open, and there would be no Bethany Anne in the vault.

Michael didn't leave the vault until the door opened. He would grab the chosen and become Myst, leaving when the door had barely cracked open.

He had found out from some of the new shows that there were now too many scientific devices to use this method any longer. They could just wait until the door was opened and check all kinds of signs, and he was sure one of them would spike.

Maybe it would be one of the ghost chasers.

If he weren't so tired, he might go and play with those ghost chasers—if he could figure out where they were going to be.

He could always have Carl check into their location for him. While he wanted to keep the UnknownWorld a secret, since that was best for everyone, the more he caused consternation to those who lived on the fringe, the better.

No matter how well your body felt, the years of living imprinted your mind. Those who feared death eventually felt a quiet death in bed shouldn't be feared too much. This acceptance often snuck up on one.

Living as many centuries as he had, even though he'd slept through so many decades, still caused weariness on the soul.

Maybe, just maybe, what the Family needed was a new parent —a mother, not a father.

If she was as strong of mind as he suspected, maybe he could hand off the responsibility for the world and go back to sleep—for a very, very long time.

CHAPTER NINE

<u>Military Base, Colorado Mountains</u>

Michael Mysted into the plane. With the gear down, there were plenty of options if you knew about a few judicious pinholes.

He glanced at Carl, who had apparently finished a drink and was relaxing and running some sort of research on his laptop. He had a few windows open, and there were some searches announcing their percentage of completion.

He changed his body back into a corporeal form and sat down across from Carl. The seats on the plane faced each other.

It took a few blinks for Carl to realize Michael was on the plane and sitting across from him. If he hadn't been so thoroughly wrung out from the stress of the last few days, he was sure he would have jumped.

As it was, his head just jerked up when he realized he wasn't alone.

"Carl, will you see what it would take to fly to the Baltics?"

Carl stared at him. The question had come from left field, so Carl had nothing to process it against; no previous knowledge of why Michael would want to go to Europe. As far as Carl knew, Michael hadn't been out of America for...um, *forever*.

Well, he knew he had come over from Europe, but that was in the 1700s or thereabouts. Pretty far back, in any case.

"Um, sure. Any particular country?" Carl wasn't sure what permits were required and how to get a plane from the US overseas, but he was sure the pilot would let him know what he needed to do. Frank could smooth over any issues...he hoped.

"No, I haven't decided exactly where quite yet. I would prefer Romania if we can fly in there. Probably Brasov, if they have an airport. Let me know what you find out about our options."

"Are we going to see someone in particular? Do we need to announce ourselves?" Carl was searching just a little. He knew the Family could be particular about uninvited guests, and there were always the *other* types of supernaturals one might have to deal with—although here in America it was never a problem. Michael had taken care of the pecking order some hundred and fifty years ago, and he hadn't heard a sneeze from the allied groups in his fifteen years.

Frank apparently had all major supernatural leaders on speed dial, so if Carl needed support it magically appeared...and they were "happy to do it." Carl always assumed it was because of a healthy respect, and the philosophy of live and let live. As in, Michael let them live, and would continue to leave them alone unless they broke the accords or dishonored him in some way.

Usually, if Carl received information on a problem event or something internal to another group, the leadership had already taken care of the situation before Michael ever woke.

It was always nice to hear about the problem and the solution at the same time.

Often Carl would receive requests for information from the other research people in the UnknownWorld if they were stymied. None of them wanted to work closely with Frank since he was too close to the government for their liking. They would pick up the phone to talk with him, but only if it was a choice between that or a conversation with Michael.

They really, really didn't want to have that discussion again. A hundred and fifty years wasn't long enough to forget, especially when many of the current leaders had moved up the ranks due to the massive number of positions that had simultaneously become available at that time.

Apparently, a handful of groups, mostly Weres and other quasi-humans, had come together and decided that since they had taken on a few vampires with only moderate casualties, they could gang up on Michael and either put him in his place or soak up enough damage to get rid of him altogether.

It was the first, and truly the bloodiest, Valentine's Day massacre. Well, it was February 14th, anyway. All the groups that had participated considered their present leadership the "Second Council" now, since most of the first group had suddenly become very dead by getting cut up into tiny chunks.

A few who could regenerate their wounds apparently pissed Michael off enough that he would cut a large part off their body and stake them to the ground so they couldn't escape until their body parts grew back, then cut those parts off again.

He had made the new pack leaders watch, to make sure they got the message that to attack him had dire consequences.

It had made an impression—one which had apparently lasted a hundred and fifty years.

Michael pursed his lips and decided to tell Carl what he wanted to know. "No, there are no families I wish to interact with. This isn't something they need to be aware of, and any of the dishonored we meet will be dealt with. I would prefer none of them were aware of our presence since it will cause too many questions."

Michael looked out the window of the small private jet. He

knew that at this instant the plane was being surreptitiously snooped on as much as possible by the military. While Carl took care of his responsibilities very well, Michael's plane was prepared to withstand all sorts of attacks—both overt and clandestine.

Regardless, you couldn't be too cautious, so Michael just projected his thoughts into Carl's brain. It was impossible to snoop there.

"You need to be careful, and protect our information as much as possible. This won't be a normal trip. We will be going into the Baltics for a week at least, maybe two. We need two additional scouts to help us into the mountains, and I will need a satellite phone to contact you about the second stage of the operation."

"I won't be staying there?"

"No. I need you to lead anyone following us on a merry chase until you hear from me. No one can know of the plan. If anyone suspects anything, that area will be crawling with dishonored and all types of supernaturals."

Carl looked perplexed for a minute. *"Why?"*

Michael sat back and looked pensive as he stared out the plane's window.

"Because a mother is to be born. In pain she will be conceived, in fire she will be tried, in agony she will be tested, and for love she will kill. Unfortunately, there is a great need to show love right now."

Carl looked at Michael for a moment, then noticed that one of his windows had a blinking red "Query Complete" at the top.

It sounded like Michael had selected his latest child. No, that couldn't be right. He had called her a mother.

He wouldn't marry, would he?

"Fuck me sideways." Bethany Anne had a bit of a potty mouth. She knew it, her father knew it, and at times like this, there wasn't a damn thing she could do about it. Besides, her dad had taught her some of her favorite phrases.

Bethany Anne believed cussing was an excellent way to release stress, and should be morally approved.

She sat for a while, a little introspective after taking in everything she had just been told.

They had mysterious people, ops so black she'd never heard about them, and government officials who could reach into her group and make up orders to send her across the nation at the drop of a hat.

Freaky and weird? Check.

Supernatural situation and unexplained invisible old geezers? Check and check.

Well, that wasn't really fair. Dad hadn't said the guy was a geezer, just older and in a suit. Spoke in a clipped fashion. English wasn't his first language, she was sure.

She wouldn't forget the "dying but not dying" part, either. She might be able to give old Hoary Long-scythe a royal middle finger, but at what cost? That was her question right now.

All of it was tied up in some sort of honor and belief system that went back way before she had been born.

She let out a long sigh. "Dad, if I'm possibly going to die but not die tomorrow, how about we play hooky this one time and go have dinner? On me? We can charge it to my American Express, and they can eat the bill."

He looked at her blankly, then cracked a shit-eating grin and stood up from his seat.

He reached for his hat. "Hell yeah, Bethany Anne. Tell you what; there's this steakhouse outside the base that has a wine cellar with some very old favorites I've been tempted to try, but didn't want the bill. That sound about right?"

Bethany Anne looked up at her father, whom she might not

see again after tomorrow. "You know what? I've got the company's Amex and a personal Black Visa that just came in the mail two weeks ago. I've been saving it for a special occasion. Let's crack every bottle they have."

Patricia's eyes grew wide as they walked by, and her jaw almost hit the ground.

Both Reynoldses were smiling...and looked like they were about to get into some mischief.

Dr. John Evenich was outside the vault, and the General's daughter was getting ready to go inside. Five other soldiers surrounded the rather small area. She was a bit of a beauty, with that black hair. A bit of a hard-ass, too. The looks might have come from her mother, but the attitude was all her father.

She was talking with her dad matter-of-factly. If he hadn't known any better, he would have sworn the General's nose was a little red. Drinking? No, probably crying when no one could see. The rumor was, he had just found out his daughter had a rare blood disease that had a high mortality rate.

They both seemed to be in good spirits, and that was just...odd.

"General...Dad, I have no idea where I'll be going or what I'll be doing, but I want you to know I wouldn't have had this chance without you preparing me the way you did. If I were a schoolteacher, this opportunity wouldn't be available right now." She looked him straight in the eyes to make sure he understood her message.

Lance, realizing she was right, considered his response. She didn't want him going through the heartache when she "died" as he had with her mother. And she was right—without him training her the way he had, she wouldn't have been prepared for this commission, such as it was. He was still going to miss her.

"I hear you, Bethany Anne. Know I won't go all Houdini's wife on you, but drop a line if you can?"

She smiled. After Harry Houdini died, his wife had performed a lot of séances to try to talk to him in the afterlife.

With a kiss for his cheek, she went into the vault, slapping the red button beside the door as she stepped in.

The klaxon went off, and the vault door started to close.

"Fuck me! No lights." The lights had gone off when the door shut. That was unexpected. You couldn't get any darker than that.

A deep voice, not unpleasant, came out of the inky blackness. "That's because I like to know the mettle of the man or woman I'm going to communicate with, and being in the dark is the easiest way to get past their defenses."

She jerked upright, her heart pumping a little faster, as she tried to figure out where in the little vault he might be.

"Bethany Anne, you might as well sit down. Reach to your left, and you will find a chair."

"You have me at a disadvantage." She reached down and found the chair's back. She only slightly banged her leg against a table as she sat down. "Who am I speaking with?" Given the direction his voice had come from, he was probably at the other end.

"My name is Michael, and I am the one who may be offering you a potential way to continue your effort to help others. My family has been working behind the scenes to help this country's military handle hard and dangerous cases—cases you will never hear about in the media. It is a lot of responsibility, to help those who cannot know they have been helped. This is similar to helping those who have passed away, true? Does this interest you?"

His voice made him sound older; cultured, but *ancient* at the same time.

"I don't know yet. Well, not true. Yes, I want to help others who need it, but I have questions. How do you expect to get out without anyone seeing you? Why do you believe you can fix what no other doctors here in the States can? Are you with a special ops group? Special Medical Testing?"

"No. Well, nothing you would understand. There are some facets to the Family that are like these groups you are familiar with. However, the reason I know you can be cured is that I've worked with and studied blood and blood issues for most of my adult life."

"Oh? How long would that be, Michael?"

"Well over a thousand of your years, Bethany Anne. Your kind might call me a vampire, but that isn't entirely true—at least for me. For my children, maybe, and certainly for their children.

"Our blood changes us, and will change you. It will remove the bad things going through your body that your doctors cannot fix. You will, in all ways, have a body superior to what you have now."

"What's the downside to going through this procedure?"

"Unimaginable pain."

Bethany Anne had expected something crazy from this situation, so although she was certainly spooked, she could only die once, right? In for a dime, in for a dozen.

"So...if you're not *exactly* a vampire, what are you?"

"Bethany Anne, I've been waiting all day for you to ask that. I am..."

Thirty minutes later, base air control gave approval for the unique civilian plane to taxi. The plane's stated destination was the East Coast.

While the plane was ramping up her engines and running final checks before starting down the runway, the klaxon startled everyone, and the vault door opened. There was a buzz of excited conversation when everyone realized Bethany Anne wasn't inside the room...and the knife was missing as well.

She was right, the General thought; she was going to leave her way. Good thing it had worked out. It would really have sucked to reimburse a $32,000 bill for one night of drinking on her existing salary. Good thing her life insurance was paid up.

Smiling to himself, the General took the prepared envelope Kevin was holding and taped it to the door. Lance Reynolds stared at the red button, something his only daughter had touched just a few minutes before, and gently pushed it. He turned around and started the walk back out of Level Five.

He chose to think of this event as a mission that had an undetermined length of time associated with it. She wasn't gone; not to him.

Kevin, Dr. Evenich, and the other soldiers just stared at the empty vault. No one knew what to say.

Ten seconds later, a gruff and annoyed General called, "Kevin! Get your ass and everyone else we have down here moving!"

Then he hit the stairs, vowing to never again return to Level Five.

Washington, D.C.

Three weeks later, the group that approved Bethany Anne to receive a Black Visa was docked a few points in their quarterly review. That one night had cost them over $32,000, and she wasn't around to pay the bill. Apparently, their risk analysis program needed to be tweaked.

In Washington, Martin looked at the last charges from Bethany Anne's company credit card and smiled. If she was going out, she had sure made the company pay for it.

He closed the agency's credit card report. Yeah, she wasn't gone. The only reason Bethany Anne would screw the company like that was because she was going to return the payment—with interest. He wasn't sure how she was going to beat Death, but he would bet his savings Death was worried about her right now.

He smiled a little as he reached for the next report he had to review.

CHAPTER TEN

Carpathian Mountains, Romania

"Dammit, you know this is bitchin' cold, right?" Bethany Anne was wrapped up like a walrus and trying to stay on the trail the two mountain guides had plowed through the knee-deep snow ahead of her.

"We've been in these mountains almost five days, and I'm not complaining much. Actually, let's be fair—I'm complaining a lot." Bethany Anne adjusted the goggles that protected her eyes from the sunlight on the snow. With the infusion of Michael's—something. Blood? Hadn't seemed like it, but Bethany Anne could feel changes in herself already. And frankly, she wasn't bothered nearly as much by the cold as she thought she should be.

Michael looked at the side of the mountain, trying to remember how it had looked many centuries ago when he had traveled through this area to find the cave he was now looking for —again.

"Bethany Anne, we both know you are neither as bothered by the cold as you are suggesting or as tired as you might have been just a few days ago had you started this little excursion by yourself." Michael believed he had now figured out why there were so few females in his family.

They mouthed off…a lot.

Even when there wasn't anything to talk about, occasionally they had to fill the dead air with whatever was on their mind. If the female was incredibly intelligent and agitated and despised the term "patience" in all its definitions, it could be bad for those who had to be around them for a long period of time.

At least the trail guides didn't speak English. No need for them to try to carry on a conversation.

Michael put up with it from her since it was part of her personality, and her impatience was going to help her and no doubt the world in the future. His burden was dealing with it in the present. He surmised that his name would be slandered for hundreds of years. Those who had to deal with Bethany Anne would be taking it in vain for a long time.

History would vindicate him…or not. Either way, he doubted he was going to have to worry about it for too much longer.

He started to recognize certain peaks. They were on the right mountain and in the right area.

He spoke to the guides in their language, which had been generations old before these were born. Fortunately, they didn't hold to the superstitious ways of only a couple of generations back. If they had, these guides would never have agreed to come up here.

Too many horror stories had started in this area of the world, and for good reason.

Before Michael had sailed to America, he had come to this area again to hide the entrance to the cave. He tracked down two Weres who suffered from psychological issues. Both had hunted humans and killed them, which had led to whispers in the taverns and homes throughout the countryside. After hiding the bodies down a crevice, Michael left. The stories had been forgotten in time.

While some in the UnknownWorld probably knew them, he wasn't sure any of the different groups believed them. He supposed he could have stayed awake more often and tried to keep up to date with all the changes, but it was just too much. Too many centuries, and too many changes to overcome in the last couple hundred years.

His morality and his belief system were too strict to coexist with this world's. His was a very black-and-white system, with consistent judgments and punishments for those who broke his faith, his laws, or his rules.

For the last fifty years, he had chosen to sleep more often than not, allowing his children and grandchildren to deal with the world.

He believed one should know truth, which required taking the time to know oneself. One didn't lie about their actions, their feelings, or their thoughts and beliefs, but accepted themselves for what and who they were. Once people understood those things, their future was more assured since they wouldn't subconsciously be fighting both their enemies and themselves to accomplish their goals.

Michael had realized many centuries before that he was not malleable regarding his honor. In the last couple of centuries, it had caused more and more problems since he had killed those who had thought his honor was something to be negotiated. That it was *his* problem he would not bend or recognize gray areas.

Unfortunately, dead people didn't learn well. Michael recognized this, and, being truthful to himself, he realized death had been the correct recourse. When one was powerful and deadly enough to mete out punishment with no checks and balances, one should be careful how many times they were called upon to judge the actions of others.

It was time to sleep for possibly the final time, and bring another in at the top—one who would die striving for others, or even just for the honor of those who had already died. That was what had called to Michael when he tested Bethany Anne. Her religious beliefs were, he considered, different. He had tested her mettle, and she would die before failing in her desire to help others—those who needed her—when she could make a difference.

His accomplishment would be making her *more* than the others, to give her that advantage and so much else.

She would fight, she would make alliances, and she had the ability to think out of the box—something Michael was too set in his ways to accomplish anymore.

His family and this world needed guidance, love, and discipline from someone as powerful as he. He just didn't have it to give.

Honor demanded he provide a replacement for this world, this time, and the future world—and future times that had to come. Bethany Anne was his hope, his desire, his penance, and his reward.

Now, if she would just stop bitching so he could think.

New York City, New York

Nathan Lowell was second under Gerry, who was both the Alpha of the New York Pack and the current head of the American Pack Council for the Weres. He was presently enjoying a nice dinner in New York City, having arrived there the day before. While the town was very nice, he felt sure he would enjoy upper New York state much more, once he had finished his business for his consulting company here. Plenty of places to go camping there.

He didn't pay any attention to the extra-special service he received from the adorable brunette waitress or the spectacularly unsuccessful flirting he was the target of.

Nathan ordered his typical dinner, which included a fair amount of steak and lamb. He rather enjoyed lamb, even if many in his pack didn't. Plus, unlike a lot of them, he liked vegetables. He couldn't remember the number of times that had caused him issues. A lot of Weres thought only baby wolves ate vegetables.

Often the only way to solve the argument was to cram enough vegetables down the throat of the guy giving him lip that he gave up trying to have fun at Nathan's expense and swallowed so he could breathe.

Since typically Nathan was holding his nose shut, the choice was to swallow or suffocate.

Nathan was powerful and deadly enough to be the pack's Alpha, but he wasn't willing to suffer the politics and the constant interruptions of the other Alphas around the country. He was happy farther down in the pack, although he frankly didn't enjoy being second, either. Sadly, other wolves kept challenging him, and the wolf characteristic he possessed in spades was the absolute inability to accept losing.

It pissed him off. So, since his only other choice was to lose a challenge to a Were trying to move up the ranks, eventually he had ended up as Gerry's second. And since he didn't desire the top spot, he had never fought Gerry for it.

He still had fights now, but with every challenger who was vanquished, the next fight for pack rank came farther apart. He was respected universally across the packs for his no-nonsense practical attitude, and he had information resources that were very helpful—especially when it came to vampire interactions.

The testosterone-imbued young idiots in his pack didn't like him. Additionally, he prevented most with enough political ambition to kiss his furry ass from talking with Gerry, the council's Alpha. So, since no one but Alphas could talk to Gerry unless they spoke with Nathan first—and very few of the pack wanted to speak with Nathan—the Alpha was rarely bothered.

Gerry found it to be a spectacular situation, and he did his level best to move the responsibilities Nathan would normally carry to his third, Nirene. She took care of the pack in ways most

Alphas would if they didn't have Gerry's additional responsibilities. Furthermore, on the rare occasions anyone gave her grief, they had learned to apologize before Nathan heard about it. He would get the story from Nirene and then the offender, mostly male but the occasional female too would get a visit from Nathan.

Then they had what he liked to term a binary decision. Either they apologized to Nirene and paid a heartfelt penance for whatever actions had disrespected her office, or they suffered until they decided apologizing would allow them to live.

Two Weres had gone the distance. They had fought Nathan, thinking they could make him bend on his demand that they apologize or else. After they had both died, others started apologizing before Nathan showed up in person to request the apology.

One smartass had decided to try to avoid Nathan by driving to another state and hiding in a cabin in the woods. It had taken Nathan a week to locate him, and the rumor was that Nathan had beaten him, then made him call Nirene and beg forgiveness from her.

Once the call was over, Nathan had dropped him off at a med school dropout's home to get treatment for injuries he had suffered when Nathan beat his ass a second time. The second beating had been for running and causing Nathan to take time away from his businesses to track him down.

Gerry was one of only two surviving council members who had lived through the Weres' version of the Saint Valentine's Day Massacre. It had happened a hundred and fifty years ago when the Alphas and their seconds and thirds had come down with a case of stupidity—and paid for it. It had taken almost two years for the packs to finally settle down after all the upheaval, with so many leadership positions open at once.

Pack dynamics, normally changing every few decades at most, had suddenly changed for every pack and every Alpha, second and third at the same time. The worst of it had been over within eighteen months, but avarice, cunning, and long lives had left a few challenges remaining years after the original struggles.

The other leader who had been smart enough to survive the massacre, Thomas, had suddenly gotten a case of "dead due to stupidity" about twenty-five years later. He increasingly suffered from arrogance as he got older, and one of Michael's kids had taken umbrage to an offhand comment Thomas made regarding Michael.

"Open Leadership Position: local werewolf pack needs new Alpha. Previous one caught a deadly case of 'Mouthing Off Around Vampire.'"

Nathan didn't remember the vampire's name. He hadn't shown much emotion over the situation; it had just been "comment made, physical reply complete." The vampire relayed his message to the next highest representative, who was all ears and made no comments.

Had Thomas just kept his Alpha mouth shut for five seconds, he might still be here today.

But probably not, Nathan mused. If you went down the stupid path when you were older, you tended to stick to the path.

It wasn't impossible to kill a vampire, and depending on how young he was and who his sire was, the vampire might not be powerful personally. The vampires who weren't part of Michael's family were more of a group.

You might piss off a particular group and have a major fight on your hands, but it wasn't the same as if you had targeted Michael's family. That was a death sentence—maybe not right away, but eventually. When Michael woke up and found out about it, you were guaranteed a shorter life.

Michael firmly believed in an eye for an eye and tooth for a tooth for the death of anyone in his family, although frankly, he couldn't be bothered with making sure the deaths on the other side were limited to the one who had killed a family member.

Since his children knew the score, they would normally take care of the problem to keep the body count down.

Michael believed in the biblical philosophy of cut down the tree, burn the roots, and salt the ground so nothing would ever grow there again.

Nathan took out his cell phone and scanned through his many business and personal email addresses looking for important messages. As the CEO of a high-level internet security firm and with his hacking abilities, he had access not only to data on the internet, but also the dark net and the locations and conversations hackers kept to themselves. If he couldn't locate it in the hidden places, he had online personas he would use to find the information in corporate and governmental databases.

There were no emails for business concerns. That was nice.

Then he took out another phone he used strictly for pack business and searched on Craigslist in each of the fourteen cities that were being used this quarter. If you read between the lines, the messages made sense—and were a bitch for the NSA and the government to figure out. If anyone actually called the people, they had the items for sale or the contacts the information offered.

Nathan was in the right section for his fourth city, Los Angeles, when one of the ads caught his attention.

"The Archangel has awakened! New cherub has been picked, and the Land of the Gentiles will receive their due. Time to visit the Promised Land and take back what is ours!"

Nathan pondered that. While on the surface it was another innocuous religious nut-job message, most of the UnknownWorld referred to Michael as the Archangel and any new children of his as cherubs. The Land of the Gentiles was typically America but could mean anything outside old Europe, really.

The more aggressive groups under the American Pack Council had been gossiping for weeks about the rumors. They chafed under the rules Michael had dictated, and since he was rarely around to monitor infractions, responsibility for discipline was left to the council—which was *not* appreciated.

Until you could pin down what Michael was doing and why, supernaturals would keep as low a profile as possible—except the young and the idiots. Usually, those two went together like politicians and lying.

Nathan sighed and felt the tension rising in his shoulders. Gerry had never taken away Nathan's role as the liaison to Michael's family, and for good reason. Nathan was never stupid. He could keep his anger on a very short leash around a vampire.

Michael would typically talk with Gerry over the phone after Carl had called to set up the time and phone number so Gerry could be ready and apprised of the reason. Nathan hadn't heard from Carl in a while.

Rumor was, the families were fighting again. One of Michael's favorites had been caught with his pants down and had died in an incredibly large and flaming explosion.

Nathan didn't have any real feelings for Bill, the missing vampire, except for professional respect. Bill had done his job, as had Nathan, and the few times they had crossed paths it had been respectful.

There were two types of vampires: Forsaken, and Michael's Family. Another way to think about it was "Michael's Family versus every other vampire in the world." Because the other team was pretty large, most werewolves chose to work with the dishonored, believing them to be the winning team—if not right now, eventually.

Nathan, however, had enough contacts across the world to realize the fight was fairly even. It was more about quality versus quantity. But even one loss, like Bill getting taken out, was a hit on Michael's family—kinda like your hockey player being put in the penalty box for a game or season.

So, enough rumors and the betting man—or wolf—assumed Michael was awake and had personally chosen another child.

A lot of supernaturals had been secretly talking about how they could eventually either take out Michael's Family or hurt them enough so Michael's rules for the UnknownWorld would become irrelevant. They would talk tactics such as going after the top children, the most powerful.

Good strategy to become instantly dead, was Nathan's opinion.

Even though Michael's Family kept the evil ones in line, a lot of people just didn't like knowing there was an ultimate authority figure with a stick up his butt about morality who had the ability to kick your ass if you didn't toe the line. Kind of like a bunch of really rich and really-powerful-but-bratty teenagers.

Nathan considered what he needed to do to find out what was going on, and how this affected the American Council and his pack.

Well, fuckity fuck. It looked like a trip to Upstate New York's forests was going to be just a dream this time.

Carpathian Mountains, Romania

Okay, Michael would admit it was a little cold. He had been searching for most of the afternoon and had found the location of the cave entrance, but not until just before dark. Since he didn't want the guides to go down the mountain at that time of day, he had mentally directed them and Bethany Anne into the cave. The guides wouldn't remember any of this.

Even with his modified body, the subfreezing temperature was a little uncomfortable.

About a hundred feet into the cave, he "suggested" the guides go to sleep. They would be good until early morning, when he would tell them to pack their stuff up and go back to the village by a different route.

At this point, Bethany Anne started to get a little apprehensive.

Bethany Anne, Michael, and Carl had talked for a while on the journey here. Carl had provided her information on the day-to-day activities he and Bill had been handling since Michael really didn't keep up with them. Carl then showed her some of the footage from a couple of takedowns and had shared the short video presentation he had made for Michael.

Michael was expecting them to make a good team. Carl was very good with the systems and had been his liaison with the other supernaturals for the last fifteen years. He knew who to talk with to narrow down the unknowns on their strikes. He had Carl provide Bethany Anne with various financial account details, and explain how to get access.

Michael hadn't really kept up with his children's families over the years. They had their areas of the world to protect, and he had Canada and the US. Well, Bill had done the traveling, communicating, and protecting until a month ago.

Michael knew something was incredibly fishy about what had been happening. Typically, the Forsaken wouldn't try anything in the States since he was so close. He *had* been sleeping, a lot, but it still never provided a good result for them.

So now he needed to outthink them, and give them a response that in their ignorance they couldn't possibly conceive.

And he had one.

Brasov, Romania

Carl was presently in Brasov, Romania. He had dropped Bethany Anne and Michael off a week and a half ago. This was old-world Transylvania. He would sit on this tarmac for another eight hours or so, then go wheels up and head toward England. He had received a couple of beeps on his satellite phone four days ago from Michael, letting him know they had reached the location.

Carl had a couple of contacts he wanted to touch base with in London. Since he was on the company's time and had a few days to kill, he decided he might as well fly where he wanted first. Sometimes, just sometimes, this job was too good to be true.

Carl didn't know exactly how Michael made children. As he understood it from Bill, Michael was the patriarch of all vampires, not just his family. Michael was at the top, with his six children beneath him. Two had fled the Family many centuries before and were the patriarchs of the dishonored.

Bill had been chosen by Michael back at the end of World War II, although he'd had one of his children transform Bill. Bill had no idea why, but he was incredibly powerful for a vampire.

His sire Stephen was Michael's third child, responsible for the area in and around the Mediterranean. He was probably the second most powerful vampire in the world. Stephen was eighty percent as strong as Michael, but he was a little bit more easygoing. It was one of the reasons the families around the world didn't miss Michael much.

While he was respected and even loved to a great degree, most of his children really didn't enjoy being around him. It had caused untold amounts of stress in the past. Add in the occasional problems with locals who didn't understand the children had fallen a bit from the family tree, at least where honor was concerned. They upheld it, but they at least (usually) gave you a chance to make amends.

Not so much with Michael.

A few days later, the plane was heading to London after a stop in Frankfurt, Germany.

Carl had decided to land there on a whim, to enjoy some especially good beer.

In Switzerland, Carl had taken care of financial responsibilities. He had added Bethany Anne to the accounts Michael always provided his new children. In addition to the normal accounts Bill had access to, Michael had identified three unfamiliar Swiss accounts, with instructions to add Bethany Anne to those as well.

He had provided DNA and personal information she could

verify. He knew a hacker might locate the information, so he wasn't providing it for a true thief. He recognized there was a small chance her mind would be messed up from the transformation, so it was an admittedly small test to make sure she had remained mentally functional.

In both Switzerland and Germany, Carl had activated a low-level AI program on his laptop, which he left on the plane, and used it to simulate conversations with Michael, thus keeping up appearances should anyone try to track Michael's location.

The jet didn't make it to London. It disappeared from the radar approximately halfway across the English Channel in a sudden storm, common to those waters. The search lasted three days before it was called off, but they didn't even find any wreckage. The plane had just vanished.

CHAPTER ELEVEN

Carpathian Mountains, Romania

Bethany Anne woke up slowly, trying to remember where she was. It was dark; so dark, and she felt like she was drugged. When she tried to sit up, she bumped her head.

You might want to rest for a minute. You have been under for a long time.

She laid back down, drawing on what cognitive ability she still had to think through what the disembodied voice just said.

Wincing in pain, she whispered into the darkness, "Who are you, and where am I? Am I hospitalized?"

No, not hospitalized, exactly. My nomenclature is a meaningless string of digits. You are on the surface of the planet Earth in a location called...

It all came back in a rush—her sickness, Michael, Carl, and coming to the cave on the mountain. Michael had taken her deep into a deserted area of the cave system, whereupon they emerged into what looked like a small hidden valley. After a little searching around, Michael found the metal ship under hundreds of years of detritus. The ship was obviously not from Earth. It was the same one he encountered a thousand years and more in the past.

Things had become a little clearer to Bethany Anne. While incredible, if you looked at just the facts, you would have to agree this was a UFO.

She remembered thinking that if nothing else, she had a story for her father if she should ever get to talk with him again.

Michael explained that this was where he had changed, with such pain as he had never felt in all his human years.

After a good night's sleep outside the ship, it was Bethany Anne's turn. Michael had warned her she had to survive the transformation long enough to retain her personality. If she did not, he would be forced to kill her immediately. Those who didn't were no better than the worst of humanity; just significantly stronger and with a lust for human blood.

If she made it beyond twenty-four hours, she would be past the worst of the trial. Michael told her before she went under that if she lasted that long, he would make a quick trip to the nearby resort town.

Michael had never mentioned another entity as part of the transformation.

"Water, I need water."

You don't need water at this time.

Thinking back to Michael's comment about hours, she realized she must have made it past the minimum twenty-four hours.

"How long?" Her voice was getting stronger, and she didn't feel like she had cottonmouth this time. "How many hours was I under?"

Over four thousand three hundred.

"I'm sorry, I thought you said, 'four thousand three hundred.' Did I hear you correctly?"

That is correct. There is nothing wrong with your hearing. You are not using it right now.

God, she thought, *I'm not coming out of this very well.*

Bethany Anne inhaled, ready to try the conversation again. "Let me see if I have this right: I'm still in the ship, in an enclosed 'something.' I have been here significantly longer than twenty-four hours. I am conversing with you, but apparently, it must be telepathic because I am not using my hearing. Is this correct?"

Yes to the time, no to the telepathy. I am symbiotically attached and have created multiple connections with both your physical and neurological systems. I have spent the time since you fell asleep examining your physiology, and have done my best to mitigate the sloppy programming which caused the painful transformation in the previous subject. Unfortunately, he was my first human, and I was ill-prepared to accomplish the enhancements I was instructed to perform. He was caused much unnecessary pain. I have had sufficient time to review the previous integration, so I was much better prepared for this effort.

Bethany Anne laid very still as she tried to parse everything she'd been told. There were many tangents she could take from that data dump; she needed a second to decide which direction to go. She heard her father's voice in her head, a memory from childhood camping trips.

"Sweetheart, if you're ever stuck out in the middle of nowhere, you have to prioritize. You need to be safe, then locate water, then find food."

This pretty much is the definition of nowhere, she thought. *I'm not in immediate trouble that I'm aware of, but let's figure this out.*

"Is my body in trouble?"

Negative. I have placed our vehicle in a sort of stasis. Until a few moments ago, you had lived but fifteen minutes of your personal time.

Bethany Anne was starting to get a little concerned as the hints in the conversation came together. "Wait, did you say 'our' vehicle? Are you talking about the ship or my body?"

Yes, this physical manifestation composed of organic matter.

Panic was waking her just fine, Bethany Anne thought. "Wait, I didn't sign up for having a passenger! Disconnect your plug-ins and disengage, or whatever it is you did, undo it. Michael didn't tell me he had an attached alien with him!"

Bethany Anne, that is not possible. My mission requires me to be able to support your planet in the coming altercations with the Z'terath. In order to accomplish this, I must be able to move beyond this location. This ship has been unable to translocate since I crashed here many of your years ago. I have watched what radio and television I can receive, along with the communication between aircraft if they are directly overhead. I have little knowledge of the bigger picture, and if I cannot find out what is going on, your planet is eventually going to find itself in an intergalactic war it will be ill-prepared to participate in, except as a minor footnote as a quickly subjugated race.

Furthermore, I made a calculated decision to connect to your nervous system while the transformation was occurring.

Bethany Anne felt a pang of embarrassment. *Wait*, she thought, I *don't have any reason to be embarrassed.*

Comprehension followed like a glowing cloud of flame, accompanied by anger. "Are you telling me you fucked up? Your little 'calculated decision' somehow blew up in your face?" She explored her body, looking for the connections the...voice...said it had made. *This shit*, she thought, *was going to have to end right here and right now.* "Open this damn sarcophagus!"

There are no external connections, so you can cease your examination to locate them. I didn't realize the virus used to transform your physical capabilities would affect my efforts, so now I have no choice in this matter. I am permanently integrated into your body. The transformation took my physical body and subsumed me into yours. My mind, if you will, has been modified, and I am presently integrated with your spinal cord. From here I have connections throughout...well, everywhere. I have been working for over four thousand hours to

bring you to consciousness. I don't understand enough of your motor coordination to accomplish movement, so you will need to find the inner lock near your right hand. Twist it in a circle, and the medical Pod will release us.

"Release *me*, you mean, you snaky alien symbiont. You are an unwelcome passenger, and this discussion isn't over. What can be done can be undone! If I could, I would kick your ass." Bethany Anne tried to move her arms. "You're lucky I don't really believe in self-castigation. Mostly." There had been that one guy, Matt, a one-night stand in Baltimore she still gave herself grief over.

Bethany Anne searched for the lock while directing her ire at her new roomie. Finding it, she twisted her arm to get it to unlock. The inside of the Pod started to glow.

"I am so going to give Michael a piece of my mind. Scary vampire or not, this is bullshit."

There is no one near us.

"What? Why the hell not?" The Pod finished opening and Bethany Anne, devoid of clothing and, she thought, buff as hell, got out of it on mostly steady legs. "Wait, did I say that out loud, or are you reading my mind?"

Her point of view seemed higher than before. Confused, she looked down to see if she was standing on something.

Her legs were longer as well as shapelier, and drop-dead gorgeous. Her whole life she had bemoaned the fact that her legs were stumpy. They were the only part of her body she hated.

Nope, she decided, *not giving these legs back*. Possession was nine-tenths of the law. Well, it was when your friends were named Smith & Wesson.

Well, to be fair, they could also be named Sig Sauer, Heckler & Koch, Springfield, Beretta, Colt, Sturm, Ruger, Remington, Glock, or Browning. All good friends when you were in a disagreement with idiots.

I am connected to everything in here.

Idiots that weren't inside your body.

"This shit just keeps getting better. Can you tell me what the date is? Michael said he would be back in a couple of days. How many days was I under? When did he leave?"

Michael left approximately thirty hours after you entered the Pod. He is not within the scanning range of the craft. You have been under a little over one hundred seventy-nine days. I don't know the present date. I haven't been able to connect with the craft's radio devices since the...transformation. Actually, the hours and date are largely accurate.

"What do you mean, 'largely accurate?'"

Plus or minus two percent.

She looked around the room with the medical Pod, then pulled out a bench near the wall and sat down.

Safe. Check.

"Is there any water in this ship?"

There are devices which can pull the humidity out of the atmosphere, but you don't need it.

"Why is that?" She stood up and started toward the door. If she didn't need water, then she was good for a while without food.

Because the energy your body needs is not wholly in this dimension. Part of the modifications included creating taps into the Etheric dimension from which I draw energy. This allows you to go without food and water for an extended period.

"Do I have to drink blood? Because I must admit, I'm really not looking forward to that." Maybe something good would come out of this colossal fuck-up.

Most of the time, probably not. Blood, human or other, has a connection to the Etheric as well. We have a limited direct tap. Provided you don't do anything which requires too much effort, you will not need to consume blood.

"Define 'too much effort.'"

Physical exertion for extended periods of time, significant healing, almost dying.

"Well, that provides positive reinforcement to stay safe," she muttered. The room she was in wasn't very big. The sarcophagus, or whatever the medical Pod was, had about four feet of space on all sides. The walls were white and remarkably clean, all things considered. There was also the outline of a partial circle about eight feet up on the wall to her right. There were little rectangles with rounded corners on all the walls. She decided they must be drawers of some type.

The symbiont wasn't speaking. *Probably thought he had pissed me off enough*, she thought.

She realized she needed a little more information to get her head around the situation and start planning what the hell she should do.

Michael had given her *some* information before she went under. His concerns about the attack on Bill. The attacks on his family in America had really pissed him off.

He had exclaimed that he was "quite peeved." His face had been as annoyed as if he had just had a bad cup of tea.

Talk about understated emotional empathy. Look it up on Wikipedia, and she was sure Michael's face would be the picture for it.

Nothing for it, she thought. It was time to get started.

CHAPTER TWELVE

<u>Boston, Massachusetts</u>

Nathan had gotten out of the pool a few minutes before and had taken a quick shower to wash away the chlorine. The chlorine just totally messed up his sense of smell—not to mention he didn't want to reek of *eau de YMCA pool* all day.

He was in town to discuss the cyber attack his Boston branch had thwarted this past week. The whole Boston team and three up from New York had spent most of the last eight days eating, sleeping and breathing cybernetic warfare with a group out of China against one of their financial clients. He was here to understand if they had done anything new that could be shared with his other three teams and to personally thank each of them. He was giving them all a five-thousand-dollar bonus, which he would share after he got the after-action review. Then it was a few hours out of town to go camping, and if there weren't any fools doing it on the trail, he could enjoy getting furry.

As he was getting dressed, the phone he used for pack business rang. It was an unfamiliar number, so he opened a special program that would simultaneously answer the phone and track the number and location back to the unknown caller.

"Nathan here," he snapped, his voice a little deeper and gravelly. Well, maybe growly, since he hated picking up pack business.

Nonplussed, Frank replied, "Yeah, good to talk to you too, furball."

Nathan took a second to overcome his immediate desire to reach through the phone and shove a chair up Frank's ass. When his mind had cleared enough to think it through, he answered, "Hello, Frank. I can't say it's been too long. Another thirty years wouldn't be long enough." He put on his headphones and started walking to his car.

Frank admitted, "Oh, I feel you on this one. I wouldn't call, except after six months you're the only one I think I can trust on this."

He felt a little sigh coming on. He wouldn't be making it to the campsite this weekend, it seemed. He deactivated the alarm on his Mercedes GLE and confirmed it was unlocked and that nothing had been done to the car in his absence. The car started with a soft purr, and he backed out of his parking space.

"By the way, I'm feeling your love. Your tracking program is pretty good, but I think it's going to get lost up on SatCom3. I figured you might be anxious if a new number came across, but *damn*, Nathan."

"Yeah, well, if your business was being attacked by China's digital black ops and at risk for trillions of dollars, I think you might be a little concerned as well." Nathan turned onto the street and headed toward the office.

"Yeah, I heard about that attack. Even though it started in China, I think you might need to see about 'super special' connections on this one. It's one of the reasons I called you. I knew you'd try to stay neutral, but the other team isn't giving you an option."

"Really? Hmm. One sec." Nathan muted the line, grabbed his other phone, and hit the speed dial for the Boston office. "Tim? Nathan. I want your guys to look at all of our other clients, even those that don't ever get attacked. I have a hunch our clients aren't the target, we are. Yeah. Start the Guardian install on all clients immediately. Get with the other three offices, and everyone take someone. Make financial clients first priority, then everyone else in descending order of PR nightmare. My gut says they're trying to cause problems for us." Nathan listened for a few seconds. "Yeah, good thought. They might be trying to get us to focus on one area and then hit us in another. Take every team up to the same level, and I'll call in a few favors to get additional help. Be there in ten minutes." Nathan clicked the call off.

He picked up the original phone. "Sorry, Frank. I took your comment under advisement and gave out orders."

"No problem. I scratched your furry back, and now you're free to help me."

Nathan thought about how stupid it would be for a normal human to knowingly irritate a Were, then considered how stupid it would be for a Were to cross the main government contact. Kinda hard to dodge all the bullets all the time, but sometimes enough bullets became a "quantity has a quality of its own" situation. "Yeah, okay, tell me what you got."

"You've heard that Michael's gone missing?" Frank asked, no beating around the bush. Nathan was probably the best informed Were in the world. Just because he wasn't the Alpha didn't—in his case—mean he wasn't the best.

Nathan turned down the street leading to his Boston office, then stopped at the guard shack before driving into the underground parking lot. Pulling into the prime parking position, he stopped the car but didn't get out.

"I've heard all the rumors, but nothing my personal computer search filters return has provided anything *but* rumors. Do you have anything concrete?"

"No, but his plane went down over the ocean, and we don't have bodies for anyone in the plane. No pilot, no Carl, no Michael. For that matter, no debris and no plane."

"How do you know they were on the plane?"

"How does anyone know anything about Michael? We know the pilot and Carl were on the plane because they were on airport security cam video, and we have audio of Carl and Michael talking a few minutes before the plane disappeared."

"How did you get audio of them talking?" Nathan wanted to know if Frank was in a bad enough situation to divulge any government secrets.

"We heard them behind the conversation between the pilot and the tower before they left the tower's airspace. How did you think?" Frank, who was good at saying everything and nothing, replied.

"Well, I had hopes you'd hit the plane's windows with a laser from a satellite and listened to the vibrations." It was incredibly weak, but a plausible concept if you believed in black helicopters (which, he realized, *were* real.)

"Mmmhmm. Yeah, I got nothing on that, Nathan."

"Okay, what do you want in payment for the heads-up?"

"I need you to go to old Europe. The last verifiable sighting of Michael was in a small town out there a little over six months ago, I think. See if you can backtrack anything from there."

Nathan stared out the window for a few seconds. This just wasn't a good idea. Although he recognized the titanic power shift that would occur if Michael was truly gone, he needed to be here with his businesses if he was being targeted by anyone in the UnknownWorld right now. "Frank, I think I need to ask for another favor. Right now, as you know, I'm on the defensive. I have over two hundred clients that are bait to these...whatever-these-are."

Frank sighed. "Nathan, I know you do. You have over two hundred and fifty high-paying and high-value clients that I know about. I've got resources I can tap who can help a national security company overcome attacks by Chinese hackers. What I *don't* have is a clandestine operative I trust to sort this out. If you trust me to get you good people with maximum security clearances to help your teams out, we can get your issues resolved in a quarter of the time. Hand it off to your top guys to pass out the responsibility. My guys can handle it inside Cheyenne, or they can be placed at your offices. Tonight, if you need them."

Shit, he thought. *Frank is in a serious bind*. In four offices, he had about forty highly technical people working for him. How many was Frank willing to give him for one person? "How many, Frank? I've got an attack happening as we speak, and I'm sitting under one of my offices on the phone with you. Not to mention that Europe isn't totally healthy for an American of my persuasion."

"Nathan, you want four hundred? I'll find you four hundred in three hours."

Nathan sighed. "Well, fuckity fuck. Looks like I'm going to Europe."

Brasov, Romania

Nathan was a little jet-lagged when he arrived in Brasov, Romania. Although it was an important town with history going back to the Neolithic age, Nathan hadn't visited it before in his travels.

He grabbed a bus heading up to Poiana Brasov, a nearby winter resort area which was one of the most popular for tourists. That was where Frank had last been able to confirm Michael's existence.

Freaking spooky, Nathan thought. Maybe there was more to the rumor that Dracula had come from Transylvania than he had considered.

September was too early for winter, in Nathan's opinion. It wasn't supposed to get all white and cold until mid-November.

Either way, he needed to get moving. He had called the local Alpha for permission to be in his area. These packs went way, way back, and could be very persnickety about other packs' members in their areas without permission. Since it was a tourist area, the discussion ended up being more of a formality than he had imagined it might, considering his position in the American Council.

Frank had provided him with information about the hotel whose security footage had included Michael. He decided he would start with that hotel and enlarge the circle. As he got off the bus, he felt something touch his senses. He stepped off as if nothing had caught his attention, and took a couple of steps forward so he didn't block the other passengers. He looked in the opposite direction from his hotel and then back again as if he were trying to find it, even though he already knew which way to go.

He saw no one, which didn't mean no one was there. It just meant they weren't amateurs. He walked toward the hotel, putting his whole body on alert while completely relaxing his muscles so they wouldn't twitch uncharacteristically and give away that he was on guard.

The hotel was typically old-school—smaller buildings with a lot of the refinements of the last hundred years retrofitted. There wasn't even a personal bath for each room.

Looked like it would be an expensive couple of days. He would pay the minimum necessary to have a personal bath, even if he had to go all the way to the penthouse. If there was anything he hated, it was sharing a bathroom. He had spent a minor fortune renovating a brownstone in the New York area just a few years ago to make sure every bedroom had a personal bathroom.

Finished at the front desk, and lucky others hadn't realized the weather was going to change so early this year, he was able to swap his reserved room for only an arm. His leg would be available for the next expensive charge.

After letting himself into his room using an old-fashioned key, he pulled a rectangle the size of a quarter and twice as thick from his grooming kit. The brown plastic device had a male audio jack on one side. He plugged it into a specially modified Android phone and clicked on a folder to bring up a special set of security programs. The selfie camera came on, and he held it to his right eye. After it took a picture, he moved it to his lips, then took his whole face.

Although earlier iterations had tried to use images as passcodes, they were quickly hacked with just plain pictures. The device he had placed in the audio jack was using technology through the camera as well as some inside the device to confirm this was Nathan, while also verifying respiration and other biometrics.

The folder opened, giving him access to programs that let him search the room for anything nasty or just plain annoying. While the phone went to work to locate anything in the digital realm, he gave the room a physical check.

He found one antique spy bug under the bedside table where a phone would have sat. He supposed the thing was from the Cold War and considered leaving it there. He thought better of that idea and shook his head—a younger Nathan would never have been so careless. He dropped the bug into a small metallic box he pulled from his suitcase—a small faraday cage. Besides, maybe the bug had history. If he found out it was used decades ago, he would have a piece of spy memorabilia.

Leaving his bag on the chair next to the bed, he grabbed his phone and grooming kit and went into the bathroom. There was a knock on the door.

Sticking his head out of the bathroom, he called, "Who's there?"

Voice a little muffled—not horribly since these old hotels didn't have great insulation—he heard a girl say, "Housekeeping. I'm here to turn down your bed, sir." She had a great accent.

He stepped over and unlocked the door. Once he was back in the bathroom, he yelled for her to come in and shut the door.

He peeked through the crack in the door and caught the profile of an attractive blond. He made the appropriate noises and paid attention to his phone while turning on the water.

After about forty-five seconds, she called that she was finished and the door shut. Immediately, his phone got a ping on one of the wireless bands before going dark again. Nathan knew they must have bugged his first room, but by changing rooms, he had messed up their plans—whoever "they" were.

He decided to finish up in the bathroom and leave the existing bug or bugs alone. She had probably bugged his bag somehow; he would have. He would have to set up a drop of clothes and other materials at another hotel and leave everything else here. He had everything he couldn't leave behind in the grooming kit, which he always carried with him.

When he left the bathroom, he could smell the perfume she was wearing—which was very strong. Strong enough to mess up his sense of smell, but not enough to completely cover the scent of a Were. He wouldn't be able to recognize her personal scent in the future, so he hoped she always wore the same fragrance.

He didn't know whether this was just a pack issue of not trusting someone at his level in their territory, something to do with the attacks on his business, or something that was going on with this business of Michael's. One thing was for sure—it had just gotten a lot more interesting.

CHAPTER THIRTEEN

<u>Carpathian Mountains, Romania</u>

Bethany Anne had found her clothes outside what she thought of the 'Pod room,' although they didn't fit her wonderfully now. Her unexpected traveling companion's ministrations had affected her physically, and she was now a little taller and leaner. Clothes that were too small beat not having any clothes.

"Is there some sort of office on this ship?" Bethany Anne winced at how she must look talking to the air like this.

Yes. Go down this hallway and take your first left. The door on the right opens into the pilot's cabin and office.

"Um, where did *he* go?" Bethany Anne seriously didn't want to run into a thousand-year-old corpse.

I believe you would call him a 'ghost in the machine' now.

She paused to consider that comment. "Are you telling me you were the pilot on this craft?"

Yes.

"And your body is where, exactly? I know your—something—is in my spinal cord, but I frankly don't need to see a body." Bethany Anne wasn't squeamish, but she didn't want a physical picture to go with the disembodied voice she heard in her head.

I had the craft break it down into its constituent parts before you woke up. I intended to hitch a ride, as you called it, a long time ago. Unfortunately, Michael wasn't a match for me, and he left before I could read the situation well. He didn't react as I had expected, and I was unable to have any sort of conversation. I hadn't been in this valley very long when he stumbled into this craft. There were no radio waves for me to listen to, so I had no way to learn about your world or your language at that time. I've only been really learning about your world in the last few decades. I've tapped into a couple of satellites, but they are mostly generic news and entertainment-related. I've understood for a while that you people find the most horrendous stories fun.

"Don't knock it when you don't know what else we go through." She was a little perturbed at the alien for criticizing human television, even though she herself thought a lot of what had passed for entertainment in the last decade was trash TV. She supposed people were able to secretly feel superior when watching the horrific train wrecks others were making of their lives on national television.

Well, she couldn't knock it too much, since her secret pleasure was watching *The Real Housewives of Orange County*. Those women couldn't seem to keep a relationship going without catfights and backstabbing...and Vicki? My God, that lady needed serious help.

If she didn't get her mind focused, she was never getting out of here—wherever here was.

She walked down the hallway, took a left and then went into the door on the right.

There was a rectangle positioned a little low for humans on the right-hand side of the door. Pushing it caused the door to slide to the side, allowing her entrance and then quietly—well, mostly quietly—it slid back, closing off the hallway. In this room, there was a round table with a translucent white glass top in the center, and a bed that looked to have been sized for a kid on the right. This was going to be like sitting in an elementary school classroom—a little cramped, but large enough.

The room was clean, but the starkly white walls seemed a little plain and made it feel like she was in some sort of hospital. Not her cup of tea.

She sat down and propped her elbows on the table, cradling her chin in her hands. It was time to sort some stuff out.

"Let's start with the obvious: is it possible to extract you from my body? I don't want to rip you apart, kill you dead, and stomp on your grave anymore. Well, not as much, anyway, and I believe in another couple of days you will be safe enough."

Yes and no. It might be possible to do, but not using any science this world has available. It can probably be accomplished on a few of the worlds of the Entarian race. They have amazing medical technology.

"Okay, but I have to get a spaceship and fly *how* far?"

Well, billions of miles. I don't remember exactly where they are, and I've not tried to translate any of my knowledge of the galaxy to what your scientists have labeled those areas in space.

"What was your purpose for coming here?"

I was selected by my race as a vanguard. A scout, if you will, to locate other potentially sapient species, and make modifications to your physical beings so that you would be capable of joining the extra-galaxy war on our side.

"What the hell? There are enough of you bozos out there that you have to get into neighborhood fights? I thought scientists had very considered opinions that if a race had attained enough knowledge to travel the universe, it would have surpassed the need to be violent? What happened to that?"

Your scientists are hopelessly naive, unfortunately. It doesn't matter if a few generations seem pleasant enough. If the genetics for mayhem aren't stricken from the DNA pool, they come back around with a vengeance, and then most of the

race doesn't have the constitution to fight back, and the violent ones win. They take the whole race and make it part of their personal war machine. Those of the race who had any inclination toward violence are able to act on those feelings, and it just feeds on itself. Violence is a disease a race must stamp out lest they consume themselves and others.

"What happened to your race? You've been gone so long. Is there anything left?"

My race, the Kurtherians, are unfortunately most likely still around, since we are an offshoot of the most terrifying, meanest, and most violent race out there. We achieved over twenty-two generations without the violence gene showing itself, which allowed us plenty of time to become masters of science and technology. We became aware of more than the normal dimensions and were able to send out scouts to distant galaxies.

Thinking ourselves wise and believing we could shepherd other beings into our own enlightenment, we sought additional subjects to help. When we realized it was possible to help other races, the political body we formed to help these races move up to a higher level we named shepherds.

Unfortunately, some shepherds were in fact imposing design specifications on the growth of the subject species or manipulating the species' DNA to create new beings in their idea of perfection. We realized violence is not always physically obvious, but its intent is.

There were twelve shepherd groups; I guess you would call them clans. They started bickering amongst themselves. At first, it was over somewhat harmless philosophical differences, but after a handful of generations, these disagreements got out of hand. Seven of the twelve broke off and formed an opposing group, which then worked to bring their races to maturity to use them to overcome the remaining five.

One clan, mine, believed this internecine war was inimical

to the future. We secretly agreed to leave a shell group to struggle with the seven as a front, hiding that a lot of us had left to look for a way to circumvent destruction by the seven. We weren't prepared for strife at that time, and frankly we probably still aren't, as it isn't in us to be violent. We had found and removed the genes from our DNA, so we weren't able to return violence for violence.

The group that left has two different strategies. One focused on extracting our essence to the Etheric. The feeling was that if we were able to move to that plane, we couldn't be attacked through the physical realm. The other was to locate a sapient species far enough away from our struggle, one whose evolution we could benefit so they could help themselves and us in a fight against the other seven clans.

There were thirty-four scout ships, and none of us shared which direction we would go. That way, if any of our clan left behind were questioned, no one would know the answer. Each ship had enough supplies and each pilot had enough knowledge of the manipulation of the Etheric to support their continued existence, so long as the ship was capable of travel.

On my third jump through a solar system I arrived too close to a wormhole, and immediately and randomly hit the jump button. Normally, it takes what you would call a few hours to line up the path to jump to a planned destination. However, the gravity from the wormhole was causing my craft to tumble, so I hit the button before it broke apart. I came out close to what you call Venus, on a trajectory that would take me by this planet. The computational capability of my craft recognized a life-sustaining world and I needed to check on the structural integrity of my craft, so I set course to land here.

I didn't realize I had problems until I was too far into your gravity and it became obvious I had to land or the craft would suffer a catastrophic breakdown.

Your planet's gravity was substantially higher than I was

accustomed to. It affected my piloting ability, and with the issues I was already having, the landing was hard enough to break a couple of pieces of equipment required to get back off the ground. Your technology, at the time, was not sufficient to make any repairs. I could not leave my craft, so I took the chance to integrate myself with a sapient member of your race. However, I failed to take into account *his* reactions. Apparently I had too much hubris, and I've had a thousand of your years to consider my failure.

"You told me you didn't have a name, but a long string of numbers. Why is that?"

No, I said my nomenclature was a meaningless string of digits. The true answer is that we refer to ourselves as the answer to a mathematical formula. We see perfection in math, and often will research for personal reasons and strive to solve a single formula. Since we tend to get fixated on that formula, others call us by a string of digits that approximate its meaning.

"Well, while I'm sure that's fascinating to a math geek, I can't call you 'Number One' or anything. Have you found a name from listening to our television or radio signals that speaks to you?"

I'm familiar with one of your mathematicians, Thales of Miletus. He was possibly your world's first true mathematician, and someone I can associate with.

"Great, an early Greek mathematician? While I haven't heard of him, that isn't a ringing endorsement of my history of mathematics knowledge. I'm not terribly fond of Thales or Miletus, so I'll call you 'TOM' as a shortened version."

"Tom?" Isn't that a short version of "Thomas?"

"No, it is an acronym using the first letter of each word of the name you supplied, Thales of Miletus—T.O.M."

I understand. I accept TOM as the shortened version.

"So, *TOM*, I'm not trying to be a bitch here, but let's talk about the Ontarians you mentioned before. Are they part of the seven or part of the five?"

It is "Entarians," and they aren't in either group. The Entarians are another race we located in the same neighborhood as the war between the seven and the five. While it is possible they have not been found yet, a lot could have happened in a thousand years.

"Figures. Okay, I'll have to put off the whole 'TOM extraction' thing for the foreseeable future, but don't think I'm okay with what you've done here. I'm not just going to accept you jumping aboard, and I *will* be extremely bitchy about this. You, in fact, are going to become my number-one target when my cycle comes each month."

Are you referencing what your female anatomy goes through during your ovulation cycle? If so, that won't happen anymore. You won't have a period or suffer from mood swings.

"Really? Un-fucking-believable! That alone just got you out of the dog house. You may sleep on the couch instead. This is looking up already!"

Bethany Anne, how am I supposed to sleep on a couch without you doing it? It's your body.

"Figure of speech. It means that while you are still in trouble, it isn't as bad as it was."

I've heard the term but didn't realize our relationship was such that it was relevant.

"Yeah, well, you're here, I'm stuck with you, you don't pay rent, you want to be carried around, and I can't get rid of you. That's pretty much the definition of a shitty boyfriend, so I think it applies pretty fucking well."

TOM decided silence was the better part of valor. If he had to make the decision again, he would do it—but he might be a bit more circumspect about how he woke her up.

"All right, TOM, is there anything on this craft we can use, and can it be fixed? I need to get back out into the world and find out what the hell is going on. Michael isn't back, I don't know where Carl is, my dad is probably a nut case right now, and let's not even discuss that Martin probably thinks I've kicked the bucket."

This craft is repairable. Certain parts need to be replaced or adjusted, but I have the specifications for them in what you would call a computer. We will need to take that along if you want access to that information.

"Yes, I want access. It isn't too big, is it? Does it require special connections or energy?" Bethany Anne stood up—that chair was too damn small—and paced the compartment. Five steps forward, turn around at the door, five steps back to the wall and repeat.

No special connections for energy, since it predominately uses the host's body heat as necessary or occasionally pulls on the Etheric connection through the host if it is substantially taxed. As to how big it is? It is quite tiny. Well, mostly tiny.

Bethany Anne thought the ensuing silence was peculiar silence, as if TOM had suddenly had insight into a situation and his mouth had come to a full stop. She stopped pacing and thought back to what he had told her. "TOM, you didn't really explain how I would carry the computer. You said no special connection was needed, that it used the host's body heat. What aren't you telling me?" She could almost hear a mental sigh between her ears.

The computer has to become a part of the host's body to communicate. The Pod would make a small incision behind your ear and place the device there. I will direct the Pod to create connections between the computer and your mind, and heal the wound.

"Are you telling me I'm going to be directly connected to yet *another* voice in my head?" Bethany Anne's voice started to attain the frosty tone TOM now realized meant she was angry.

Yes.

Bethany Anne stood still for a few minutes, trying to get her annoyance under control. She wanted to kick something, preferably Michael—if he would just show up. The more she thought about it, the more she was beginning to think Michael had taken a sabbatical. It was possible it had been enemy action, but how likely was it that Michael had found somebody here in his child's area who could truly harm him?

A little self-doubt crept in. If Michael was dead, then she was both figuratively and literally out in the cold—and if anyone was looking for Michael, they would probably off her as well. She knew enough to realize that while all his children had been made by Michael, he brought *her* to the source. The original creator. And now she had the freaking creator living within her. What a cockup.

Then again, she knew everyone was either outright afraid of Michael or had great respect for his strength and ability to cause untold mayhem.

Well, that, and his honor was touchy as hell.

That meant she wasn't going to be able to just go out and discover what the hell had happened by asking the first non-human she could find. There was no telling who was behind the attacks. Michael hadn't known before he left, and she knew Carl didn't know. She tried racking her brain for the name of that government connection. Ah, it was Frank! Well, fat lot of good a name did her when she couldn't remember any other contact information.

Besides, how exactly would she find a non-human? She needed more intel. She needed an edge.

Dammit, she was going to need that computer.

Fuck my life, she thought.

CHAPTER FOURTEEN

<u>Brasov, Romania</u>

Nathan left the hotel and decided to walk to the local tavern. While it wasn't a great plan for finding Michael, it *was* a good way to get a beer. Or, considering the cold, something that would warm him a little better.

He stayed on high alert for the few blocks he walked to the tavern, where a sign out front proclaimed a wide selection of ales available. Nothing triggered his senses.

When he entered, a bell rang over his head. About a dozen people were enjoying a late afternoon beer. There were a couple of guys drinking together at the bar at the far end. A pretty bartender caught his eye as he came in and raised an eyebrow. He motioned that he was going to set up at the other end of the bar, and she came down with a rag and wiped the area as he sat down. He noticed it didn't look like it had needed a wiping, which was nice.

"What you want?" She had an honest expression, with no hint of guile he could see, and remarkably blue eyes. Her voice had a beautiful lilt to it from her Romanian accent. Nathan could have listened to her read a tax book aloud for hours.

Having strategically set himself up so he could see who came through the door in the mirror behind the bar, he asked her for a local ale—not too dark—and to surprise him. A quick smile and she was off to pull his drink for him.

Not even a minute later she returned. "Not too dark, yeah?" Her smile was too damn pleasant to have been behind the bar for many years. Either that, or he'd lucked into a great pub.

He nodded his thanks and asked for a menu. While he *could* speak Romanian, it wasn't generally known—and he preferred to keep it that way. He pointed to a picture of a bean-paste soup with smoked meat, known as *Iahnie de fasole cu afum*ătură.

Good thing he liked vegetables.

He had just bent over to start eating when he caught the scent of an UnknownWorlder. It was some sort of Were creature, and freakishly powerful. It wasn't necessarily in the building, so it was probably on the clothes someone was wearing. He looked around, using the mirror each time his head came up after taking a spoonful of the soup. There were a couple of guys together at a table near the back, with a couple of beers apiece. They seemed to have been there for a little while, and judging by their clothes, they had been out in the country.

He caught the attention of the bartender and motioned that he was going to the restrooms in the back. She nodded and kept cleaning the bottles behind the bar.

He walked slowly toward the restroom. The smell was stronger back here. He caught a little of the pair's conversation and was able to understand they had been fishing up in the mountains for the last few days. When he passed them, he confirmed that the smell was on their clothes.

The Were, whatever it was, must have checked them out while they were asleep and decided they weren't a threat.

Coming back out of the restroom, having washed his hands twice, he picked up a little more. They were discussing tracks near their camp, probably those of a huge brown bear.

Well, that would be about right, Nathan thought. While he didn't know any werebears himself, there were a couple up near Canada who interacted with the American Council.

Nathan figured that if anything had happened in this area, this Were would know. But how, he considered, was he going to get an introduction to a bear?

Ecaterina watched the new customer out of the corner of her eye. He was obviously American, and obviously not a typical tourist. His clothes, while not flashy, were high quality, and he walked with a grace that suggested a hunter; more than just a game hunter. No, this man hunted other people, evidenced when you watched him keep everyone under careful surveillance using the bar mirrors.

She had caught his eye when asking for his drink preference, and for a moment his eyes had seemed to change; to be more than human. It was disconcerting, but by the time she had drawn his ale, she had decided that it must have been a reflection from the glass.

Then again, she had seen enough in the mountains nearby to think that maybe the old stories had more truth in them than the new generations wanted to admit.

Her family had been in this area for the last seven generations; they had come from Germany to work. Although she was presently tending bar, her real skill—one passed down to every member of her family, male and female—was out in the mountains.

Cali and Alin had just come back from a desolate area and had mentioned seeing the huge tracks of a brown bear. While brown bears were well known in this area, most people had not seen large ones. She herself knew of one because she had often tracked on the mountain it called home.

She loved her family and loved the mountains, but she had a desire to see what was on the other side. Some called it a curse since the need sometimes caused unhappiness. But she had a desire to see and do more. She was happy enough right now, but she wouldn't stay here forever.

She had not dated much and had never been seriously involved with any guy. She didn't want any more ties to this area. She *would* come back, but she already knew she wasn't going to stay. She wondered why she was so interested in this man. What was he to her plans to leave Brasov? Would he be a trap to keep her here?

Only one way to find out, which was to learn more about him.

As he sat down again, she drew him another draft. He wasn't quite finished with his first, but the owner wouldn't mind if he didn't pay. Most guys took it as a favor when she proactively brought them another round. The few who turned it away were a small loss compared to the many extras she got guys to purchase.

She caught his eye as she came up to him, trying to size him up as if she were out in the mountains, following the tracks of an animal.

Nice, big, good-looking animal, she thought. She smiled without forcing it.

"You want to try another ale? Maybe something that would go well with the soup?" She set the cold mug, a drop of froth coming down the side next to the almost-finished first mug and raised her eyebrow.

He pursed his lips and looked down at the second mug. She kept her hand on it and waited patiently. Ecaterina knew patience, whether she was waiting for an animal she was tracking to break cover or a man deciding whether he was buying an ale, a smile, or a chance at a contact number.

"Depends," he replied. "Can I ask you a couple of questions if I buy that ale? It looks good, but I didn't ask for it."

Damn, she thought, not going to be easy. *Well, challenge is good.*

"Yeah, probably. So long as it has nothing to do with what time I get off or my phone number." She took away the sting with a twinkle in her eye and a smile.

He looked hurt, but the answering smile at the corner of his lips gave his playacting away. "Okay. So I'll think of two completely different questions, fair?" He reached for the ale, forcing Ecaterina to either accept the deal or pull the beer away.

How had the hunter become the hunted? she wondered. Well, you can always come around and catch them from the back.

"As you Americans like to say, 'shoot.'" She took his first mug away and wiped the bar down.

"I'd like to go out and see some of the mountains. Do you know anyone who could help me find my way around out there?" He kept his eyes on hers as he took a pull on the mug, then broke eye contact to look down at the beer. "Hey! This is really good. Why didn't you suggest it the first time?"

"Is that your second question?" She smiled at him, raising her eyebrow again.

The man seemed nonplussed at that question, and looked down at the mug and back at her. His smile reached the heavens, and the stars were alight in his eyes. "Okay, you got me there. How about I buy one more of these and I get three questions?"

"Possibly. Let me hear your second question, then maybe I decide if you need another mug, yes?" One should always know what type of bait to use, her papa would say when he taught her about the mountains.

"Okay, fair enough. Is there a way I can get outfitted to stay out in the mountains for two, maybe three days? I just need to rent, not to buy, and I'd like to use something from someone who goes out all the time. I prefer quality equipment."

"Okay, you need to buy another mug while I make a phone call. When are you interested in leaving?" Ecaterina needed her brother to negotiate price with this man. It was always smart to let someone who wasn't involved and didn't have a stake to front your business effort; she could tell she was too intrigued right now to make a smart call. Ivan would do a good job of checking him out. She always checked out the women for Ivan when he did any transactions, and he returned the favor. What was family for? Well, that, and Ivan wouldn't go and rat to Papa and Mama that she was considering taking this American out on the mountain alone.

While Papa understood she could just leave him out there and she could take care of herself, her mama would give her a handful of reasons she would have to either marry him or go to the nunnery the very next day.

Mama was a handful, and Ivan was smart enough to keep their transactions quiet. If he wasn't, payback would be a bitch.

The man pursed his lips as if thinking it through. "Say, right after breakfast tomorrow?"

She nodded in acceptance of the information, threw the towel over her shoulder, and walked to the other end of the bar to call Ivan. It took everything she had not to look over her shoulder to see if this guy was checking her out.

Just because she didn't get into any serious relationships didn't mean she was unaware of how the game was played. She called Ivan's number, and he picked up on the second ring.

She spoke to him in Romanian, not too loudly, and explained she needed him to come and talk with an American about taking him out to the mountains and renting him gear—probably Ivan's gear since it would fit.

Ivan said he would be there in half an hour. After hanging up, she pulled the third draft and walked back. Setting the beer in front of him, she explained a man named Ivan would be there in thirty minutes to discuss the trip and the rental with him. He accepted the mug graciously and watched her walk away. She didn't need to look over her shoulder this time. She could feel his eyes tracking her.

CHAPTER FIFTEEN

Carpathian Mountains, Romania

Inside the ship, Bethany Anne was having what she termed "communication issues" with TOM. She had left his personal cabin and was using the hallways to walk and talk, so she had room to pace more than five steps.

She had taken the time to check out the rest of the craft—what there was to see of it. The main compartments were there. The cockpit was almost too small for her to fit in comfortably—no large *Star Trek*-style bridge on this ship. There was TOM's room, the medical room, which was thankfully larger, and the hallway between the entrance and the medical room. Bethany Anne had asked about that design decision, and he had explained they knew the Seven (they had become capitalized in her head now) rode species that dwarfed the original Kurtherians, so they had adjusted the size in the medical/science room and the hallways to the best of their abilities in their ships. Most of the ship was still undersized for her. Well, the *new* her, which was about five inches taller than Bethany Anne 1.0. She imagined it wouldn't have been too bad a fit before, but there was no way someone much taller was going to be comfortable in the core areas of the ship.

She had discussed their ability to fix the ship, and what its capabilities were. There were no armaments because his kind genetically couldn't even *think* about being personally responsible for the purposeful destruction of another. Why put in place what you weren't going to use?

Most of the craft was in pretty good shape. The materials had suffered no discernible rusting or any negative reaction to Earth's atmosphere that she could see. There was plenty of growth over the craft, which helped shield it from satellite surveillance, and there was only the one way into the valley if you didn't include scaling incredibly high peaks or parachuting in. Because these mountains had more than enough other areas to explore, it seemed that Michael and their guides might have been the only other humans here in generations.

She never did get the story of how he had stumbled upon it, or what he was doing in such a remote place a thousand years ago. Michael could be very stingy about divulging information when he chose to be.

She supposed that was what happened when you were the pinnacle of power for so long—you could simply ignore what you didn't want to talk about. She decided it was part of the reason he had such a dysfunctional family.

Because let's face it, he was responsible for all known vampires in the world. It obviously wasn't TOM's fault. Although he had started it all, he was stuck here. Every other vamp out there had Michael as their great-great-great-something-something grand-papa vamp.

Like it or not.

She considered he had become overwhelmed, choosing to get involved in only the most egregious situations, and letting his remaining children and their children take the battle to the other side.

Until her.

She was now the second human modified by the original

source. Michael apparently didn't want another child doing his bidding; he wanted to pass the baton. He wanted to give the world someone else with his superior capabilities who could hold their own against even his firstborn children.

The realization struck her. That bastard had gone and left her on purpose! A white-hot fury started burning behind her eyes.

"That motherfucking bastard! I'll tear off his 'nads and throw them so far away even *he* couldn't find them! I'm going to take this ship and shove it up his ass right after I slap his fucking face! So help me, I'm going to find that conspiratorial, responsibility shirking, morality judging fucktard and sit on his back while I rip off one arm at a time and beat his head in! I cannot believe he fucking left me here *alone* to clean up his mess!" She emphasized every comment by punching and kicking the wall, her temper masking the pain for the moment.

As her anger started to subside, Bethany Anne finally truly looked at the walls and realized that her hands were bloody and there were sizable dents in the metal, along with one or two holes into the rooms behind them.

It looked like not only was her anger a bit more intense than before, but the damage she could inflict was potentially off the charts now. She looked down at her bloody hands. She could see the skin growing back over her knuckles, and while some pain remained, it helped her to snap out of the tantrum and wasn't debilitating.

Trying to slow her breathing, she asked in an alarmingly calm voice, "TOM, how much energy did I just use?" She was starting to think that maybe this temper tantrum was going to require a disgusting karmic response.

You have depleted sixty percent of the reserves.

"So, no bloodsucking right now?"

No.

Well, she thought, that was a small favor. Considering the

damage to the metal wall, even as thin as this metal was, she was going to have a hell of a right hook.

"How long to get the reserves back?"

Probably twenty-four hours to get you back to where you were, but I haven't ascertained the maximum for you at this time. I cannot calculate your maximum.

"Okay, since I'm healing already and probably need to get a onceover, tell me how to get the computer installed and how to set up the Pod-doc to handle it since you aren't this machine's ghost anymore."

He directed her to the engineering compartment in the back of the ship.

After retrieving the small dark-green lattice-looking material from the engineering area, TOM had her place it in a small compartment in the medical Pod. He walked her through how to turn it on, and what symbols and buttons to push as they lit up on the glass surface. Not having a clue what any of it meant was annoying, but she trusted that TOM was now as personally invested in her wellbeing as she was…if for different reasons.

She hadn't stopped thinking about the potential for the "infamous Seven," as she thought of them to bring their pissing match to her neck of the universe. TOM couldn't tell her exactly how far away they were since the onboard computers didn't have any navigation information available for this part of the galaxy. It had been expected that he would have mapped his way through the unknown areas, and therefore have the necessary information to find his way home—pretty much how cowboys would ride and occasionally look behind them to help them get back again.

TOM had obviously skipped too far. He hadn't had any decent astral cartography or enough time to take good long-range views before he had landed on Earth. Then he couldn't get back into space to get the kind of views he needed for the craft's sensors.

Not wanting to bring future worry into the present, she decided she would focus on the here and now.

She hoped.

She undressed again and left her clothes on the fold-out bench, then got ready to lie back down in the Pod.

The medical Pod was set up to handle the minor surgery. Since we do not intend to be back again anytime soon, are there any body enhancements you want to consider before you get into the Pod again? Did the new body affect you overly much? I tried to adjust according to what your DNA said was the perfect you. It wasn't like I could have asked you in advance.

"The DNA said I should have these legs? Hell, no!" She indicated her body "Leave all this alone." She thought for a second. "What options are there? You've told me about the speed, the power is obvious, and the Etheric energy—and we haven't tried tapping into that yet. I don't seem to get hungry or thirsty anymore, but I swear if I can't enjoy an Italian sausage and pepperoni pizza, I'm going to figure out a way to kick your ass. Hey, am I going to gain weight easily if I eat and am also pulling energy?"

You won't gain weight no matter what you eat. Anything you consume, I can pull energies from the Etheric to use in some form or fashion even if it is just to get rid of it.

"So wait...I can't be poisoned?"

Someone can *try* to poison you, but eventually, I could neutralize the poison and either get rid of it through your body or move the energy into the Etheric. You would suffer— possibly seriously—before anything could be done, depending on the type of poison. And if you were incapacitated, you could suffer other attacks you couldn't defend against.

Bethany Anne, as clothed as she had been the day she was born, considered her options. She was going under the knife for what she hoped was the last time.

"I don't suppose you have any options for armor?" She smiled despite herself, thinking what would happen if she got into a fight and she could turn her skin into armor.

You want to walk around in a metal skin?

Bethany Anne could hear his incredulity in her mind. Taken aback that he hadn't told her it couldn't be done allowed her to consider the potential results of always weighing hundreds of pounds.

"No, skip that, but the idea is sound. Can you do something so my body is more difficult to break if I punch through metal walls or I'm hit by bullets or something?"

Bethany Anne was starting to realize that she could almost hear a small buzz when TOM was obviously thinking hard. She waited as patiently as she could to let him think this through.

The system allows me to exchange certain amalgams of materials for what you have in your body already. We know how to rapidly change one for another using the Etheric such that your skin could just change to a metal substance. I have set the Pod to review your internal structure to confirm what can and can't be done. Your skeletal structure can most likely be enhanced by exchanging your bone structure for synthetic materials. This will take a few more days in the Pod. Is this acceptable?

"Is it going to affect my weight?"

No, the new substances are little different in weight from the bone construction you have now. However, the structure will rearrange the molecules in a significantly stronger fashion.

"How much stronger?"

It ups your bone compression capabilities, which are already good, by a factor of seven, your tension abilities by a factor of twelve and your sheer abilities, which are normally your species bones' weakest, by a factor of eighteen.

"That could be handy. Tell me what to push to make that happen." Bethany Anne went through the menu as TOM instructed, then the Pod opened again and she got in. The Pod closed, and her last thought was that she'd forgotten to triple-confirm he wouldn't change the length of her legs.

Brasov, Romania

Nathan walked back to his hotel. He had stayed at the pub for another hour and a half eating another bowl of the soup and talking with Ivan. It was obvious he was related to Ecaterina. They smelled similar.

He never gave any indication or admitted he knew her, but it wasn't a difficult discussion. Ivan's English was superb, and he spoke with an accent Nathan would kill for. He was close enough to Nathan's six-foot-four toned physique that Nathan could rent Ivan's stuff. He was surprised to find out that he was negotiating with Ivan for Ecaterina's guidance in the mountains. Apparently, she was the best in a family known for their abilities in the wild and had been all over the mountains in that area.

Ivan had driven a hard bargain to rent his admittedly high-quality gear, but Nathan had been absolutely screwed on the amount he was paying for Ecaterina's help. He could only appreciate how Ivan had let slip who was taking him into the mountain at the very moment he had mentioned the daily price—no partial days—so Nathan's mind went to the very attractive bartender, who not only enjoyed being out in the wilderness but was one of the best in the area. His inner animal really was excited about the possibilities, and he had just agreed without doing a conversion of the requested amount to American dollars.

He now calculated that he just paid her approximately six months' wages for two to three days in the mountains. He hadn't been so obviously out-negotiated in...well, decades. While his wallet was hurting, his heart was happy.

He picked up that feeling of being watched as soon as he exited the pub. Surreptitiously, he adjusted his gear and caught a familiar perfume on the wind. Well, he had one pegged. He didn't look around to find her; knowing he was clued in was enough for him right now. The question was whether this was just a quiet surveillance op or something else. Keeping his senses on alert, he walked back to the hotel.

He arrived back at his room, and once inside started pulling his gear from holsters and pockets. He checked in with his teams back in the States. The people Frank had provided, an additional four hundred over his existing forty, had been able to reduce the implementation time for all his clients substantially. They had caught one client who had just come under attack, and it had taken only a few hours to win that fight. All clients were now under his new Guardian Project protection, so he thought they were going to be good for the next two quarters at a minimum. If he got extremely lucky, it could take eight to twelve months for the hackers to find holes his team hadn't found and patched proactively.

His other businesses were all relatively tiny and inconspicuous. The rest of his business efforts were local, except restaurants here and there that he was a silent partner in and a few installations and blue-collar businesses his partners ran. He also ran a big real estate effort run through a couple of shell corporations that should hide his involvement, unless one of the state agencies took it upon themselves to get interested in him. Typically the UnknownWorld wouldn't get involved with the government beyond what they were doing there in America, but the non-Family vamps in South America and Africa were known to become closely connected to the more despotic dictators. Third-world-country politics didn't usually bother the major powers, and if something curious was mentioned in their newspapers that seemed unbelievable, the powers that be didn't get involved since their constituents couldn't locate the country on a map.

He connected his security apps to the sensors he had left

behind, and they confirmed no one had been in his room since he'd left to go to the pub.

He considered whether it was safe to sleep in the room that night. So far, his watchers were being circumspect, and while he had talked with Ivan about trekking, that wasn't a strange request for someone like him. In fact, it probably would have been more telling if he *hadn't* tried to get out into the wild at some point. Doing it on his first day in town was just about the best cover he could have come up with.

He knew the bear was a Were, and he could sense the age and power just from the smell he had left on the clothes. He hoped the Were hadn't gone completely over to his alternate self for too long and would be able to give him some insight into the happenings around here.

The rumor was that Michael was from here. Well, the Michael everyone knew about, anyway. It couldn't be a coincidence that Michael had brought his proposed scion into this area, but it did speak to it being remarkable. The child who lived on the nearby coast hadn't been seen in three years, so he wasn't involved in making this change.

That left only Michael as the new sire, which meant he was starting a new Family with a female as the head. This was going to be a serious change to the existing family.

Nathan couldn't have realized then how right he was—not only regarding the families, but the whole UnknownWorld. There were changes coming, and similar to Michael's requirement to follow his strictures, the Weres' choices would become swear allegiance, hide, or die.

Because according to the rumors, vampires were dead, and if Bethany Anne was, then death became her very well indeed.

CHAPTER SIXTEEN

Carpathian Mountains, Romania

Bethany Anne woke up with a splitting headache, which quickly went away.

Sorry about that. I couldn't gauge your pain levels until you woke up.

"What the hell?" Bethany Anne was getting her bearings now, waking up in the Pod for a second time.

Well, we have a little problem with the organic computer. Your species is a little complicated to connect appropriately, so I couldn't debug your interface while you were asleep. I've engaged the core functions, but we must work on the other interfaces as time permits.

"Why did I have such a horrible headache?" She reached out and turned the lock, opening the door and getting back out of the Pod. She verified her legs looked just as long as before.

Okay, she thought, *I might be a little vain here.* She went over to the bench and started dressing.

The organic computer and your synapses weren't exactly compatible, so I had to create some intermediate filters to get

you connected. Without your input—in this case, your pain—I couldn't assess if I had done things correctly.

She finished dressing, grabbed her coat, and started for the door. "So, anytime you work on the interface to the computer, I'm going to suffer?" She continued to the hatch that led outside and keyed in the sequence to activate the locks once she left.

Stopping five feet out of the craft, she slowly turned around. She would swear the area was empty. It was as if the craft created virtual camouflage from the area around it. "Why did I know how to set the security?"

Apparently, at least one of the connections related to ship's functions is connected appropriately.

Bethany Anne could hear the surprise in TOM's voice much more clearly now than before. "TOM, do you think this computer is facilitating *our* communication?" She went over to touch the ship. It was still there, but it was like touching a high-definition screen: you tried to reach into the forest, but your hand was stopped.

That is a possibility. I don't know of any experiment trying to interface one of our organic computers with another species.

Bethany Anne considered his response. She was thinking about the fact that she just volunteered to be the universe's first guinea pig between a human, a Kurtherian, and an organic Kurtherian computer.

Her normal reaction would have been to blow her top, but she didn't feel angry. What she felt was analytical. While not a normal sensation, she knew she got like this when she had worked on cases for Martin before her fateful new assignment had led her to this situation. She considered the facts that she was still alive and largely functional and had an unknown organic computer integrated into her brain with nothing negatively affecting her thinking—she hoped.

She started walking toward the cave in the cliff that would

eventually take her back out to the other side and toward the town Michael was supposed to have visited before his mysterious disappearance.

She didn't think the trip would take long since most of their time getting there had been spent walking in circles while Michael tried to locate the right cave entrance.

She found her way to the other side relatively quickly and spotted light pollution in the southeast, so she headed in that direction. The lack of light didn't stop her from seeing everything just fine. Using small-animal trails, Bethany Anne started down the mountain.

Seemed like every time she was on this mountain it was snowing.

Brasov, Romania

Before daybreak, Nathan gathered up all his sensors and put them back into their cases. He grabbed two sets of clothes and left the rest of his gear in the room. He checked carefully to make sure he wasn't taking any bugs along, then put his stuff in one of his cheap compact bags and slung it over his shoulder. He was meeting Ivan down in the hotel lobby to retrieve his gear from a storage area he rented, and they would meet Ecaterina outside of town before backpacking into the mountains to look for tracks.

Ivan, looking a little worse for wear, met him downstairs. It was obvious he wasn't a morning person.

"Sorry, I don't do too good before I drink a liter of coffee, or noon. Both would be preferable." He smiled and held out his hand for Nathan to shake.

After fulfilling the greeting ritual, Nathan adjusted his backpack and followed Ivan out of the hotel to a waiting vehicle. Ivan sat in the front passenger seat, so Nathan took the back.

Ecaterina was the driver. "Good morning!" Nathan was pleasantly surprised to see her in the car. Sliding over, he closed the door and set his bag on the seat.

Ecaterina pulled off the curb and started toward the storage unit.

"Good morning to you, too. We were never appropriately introduced. My name is Ecaterina Romanov, and you have met my brother Ivan." She steered the old Mercedes Benz through the early morning light.

"Ivan was good. I have to admit that setting me up with him to do your negotiating was a trick I hadn't run across before. Not sure about female guides around here, but I wouldn't have dismissed you out of hand if you had explained you could help me out on the mountain."

"Is, how you say, not a problem. I run into Americans who make assumptions about barmaids too many times not to find solution. Is only practical way. I do same for Ivan when he has females to deal with, since he can't seem to think his way past pretty smile and dimples. Dimples cost him very much every time." She glanced at her brother, who seemed to be a little redder in the face than the cold warranted.

"It's true," he admitted. "I would be the knight in shining armor to every pretty, dimpled face that came my way if it wasn't for Ecaterina. Fortunately, she has shown me how to be nice without being foolish. It is always easier to give back money than to get it after the job."

They turned into a narrow alley that led to a small building with a padlock on the door. Ivan got out of the car after telling them to wait and unlocked the padlock from a large set of keys. He swung open the door to reveal bags hanging from the walls and boxes on the floor. He grabbed a couple of hiking backpack rigs and started quickly filling them from around the small room.

Ecaterina spoke from the front. "Don't worry, Ivan knows what we need for a three-day hike. He will make sure there is no extra weight, but we'll have enough extra supplies if we get caught up in a storm."

Nathan, paying attention to Ivan's efforts, barely heard what she said. "I'm not worried. It was obvious from our conversation that he knew what I needed as well as I did. In fact, a little better, since he knows the conditions on the mountain better than I do." Nathan could always switch to his other form and make it out of the mountains if he had to, but that would mean Ecaterina was dead, she knew more than she should, or something bad was happening and he needed to draw the threat away—like a certain very large, very powerful bear.

Finishing the packing, Ivan grabbed both harnesses and carried them to the back of the Mercedes. He locked the storage room and got back in the car.

"*Gott Verdammt*, it is cold out here." Ivan blew on his hands.

Nathan, always warmer than humans, was only slightly bugged by the weather. He knew that in the mountains it would be more uncomfortable, but it would take a lot to make him truly miserable.

After three hours, Ivan dropped Ecaterina and Nathan off at a place close to a trail she knew. Nathan grabbed his rig and followed Ecaterina up the main trail. He realized it probably would become cold enough to be uncomfortable to him soon. What had Ivan said? Oh, yeah. "*Gott Verdammt!*"

Ecaterina watched as Nathan pulled his backpack on. Two things became immediately obvious: he was incredibly strong, since he was lifting an eighty-pound pack with one arm, and he had worn this type of backpack before. He adjusted and buckled the straps without even looking, which took a lot of previous experience.

He didn't look to be too inconvenienced by the snow and cold.

While she wasn't badly off, she had grown up around it. She waited until he was finished and took off up the trail.

Ecaterina had inquired about what he wanted to see, and he had told her he wanted to go to where the big bear tracks had been seen last. She let him know it would be illegal for him to shoot anything and he advised her he didn't have anything big enough with him that he trusted not to just piss off a bear.

She carried her rifle. While it had a large bore, she had no desire to shoot at a large bear. She might, with a lucky shot, stop a bear, but she wasn't too comfortable with trying it. It had plenty of stopping power for most of the other animals on the mountain, though, and she was a very good shot.

Ecaterina smiled to herself. She was being paid well enough for this trip to get the other rifle that was on her wish list. Ivan had played Nathan well enough that even if nothing else came of this trip, she was set until early next year. She walked ahead of him. He might as well enjoy the view, such as it was under her gear. *Follow the cheese, little mousie*, she thought.

CHAPTER SEVENTEEN

Carpathian Mountains, Romania

Bethany Anne headed for a lake about three miles away.

She had spent a little time making sure she could find the cave's entrance again, piling a couple of cairns in some not so obvious places. TOM explained he would be able to recall any images she needed. She used the trip to update TOM on everything she remembered from the conversations with Michael and Carl. He failed to inform her he could get into her memories just fine. He thought she would be a little sensitive about sharing some of her information.

She had found a grove of trees about thirty minutes from the entrance. There were many saplings, and she thought if she were to break enough of them, it would make an obvious focal point in the future. So, taking her time and starting at the smallest, she tested her ability to punch, kick, and strike trees until it was Bethany Anne twelve, trees zero. Even the four-inch-thick tree went down. The bone upgrades had apparently been well worth it. The amount of force necessary to shatter the tree would have shattered her human bones as well.

She hadn't been out in the real world for a significant amount of time. It had been snowing when she came in, and it was snowing now, so somewhere between seven and ten months was her guess. Based on TOM's calculations it was closer to seven, but until she talked with someone, she wasn't going to accept that.

She kept one of the long limbs and broke some of the smaller branches off. If she needed to defend herself it wouldn't be as good as a bō—or better yet, a pistol—but it would allow her to choose close combat if she wished to engage. Sure, she would survive probably anything the mountain threw at her, but she didn't want to waste time, energy, and annoyance fighting a cat up here and healing the scratches she would probably get, or a bear. With a good stick, it would just be "batter up."

One thing her new abilities *didn't* provide was expert guidance in choosing the right path. She had made one choice that had ended up in a blind valley, and even her superior abilities wouldn't let her go up that cliff without tools.

She had lost some time, but that didn't overly concern her. Without the need for food and water, careful planning and packing wasn't a sensitive issue.

Once the lake was in view, she estimated she was ten to fifteen miles from the town.

The wind carried all sorts of knowledge if you knew what you were smelling.

Alexi was in his bear form. He preferred it to his human one, and most of the time he stayed in it, especially during the winter. Hard to beat a thousand pounds of fur-covered fat.

The largest known brown bear in the Carpathian Mountains was around eight hundred pounds, so in his Were form, he was about thirty percent larger than any local brown bear—enough that he never had to deal with fights. When he had in the past, no animal had been able to overcome the weight and intelligence deficit.

This morning he smelled trouble. He could sense the girl who had been all over his mountain many times, but this time she had another with her—a non-human. He doubted she knew it; her scent had no flavor of the fear it would carry if she had known.

His area had been claimed by a wolf pack out of Brasov, but his mountain was off-limits. They didn't bother him here, and he wouldn't go find them and make them eat their asses for claiming his area. He hadn't given two seconds of thought to who had claimed his mountain. They could claim all they wanted; it didn't hurt his feelings. But coming onto his mountain was a completely different proposition, so this new wolf had to be investigated—especially since they were heading toward his lake.

He left his den and started toward where his niece Ecaterina liked to spend the night. Wolves could be so temperamental, he thought.

Ecaterina had been able to keep going all day. Nathan admired her ability to keep moving forward under her loaded backpack. It explained her shape and all-around excellent health.

They had stopped for an early afternoon meal; nothing cooked, just packed meats and cheeses. They drank some water and kept walking. They didn't talk much since both enjoyed the outdoors and were lost in their thoughts.

As they neared the lake, Ecaterina took him a little way up to a small clearing that provided some cover and a wonderful view. There was an area already cleared for a fire, with a circle of stones and some logs under a tree.

"You can set up your tent under either of those two trees to the right. I'll set mine up under this group here." She pointed toward a nice spot under some pine trees.

Nathan considered his reply, then just nodded in agreement. He might want to find out more about this woman, but being forward was probably not the best option. He was sure many guys had made that choice…and failed miserably. Besides, he needed to figure out how to contact the owner of this mountain. He had been smelling him for the last two hours, so he knew he traveled here often. With the wind at their backs all morning and afternoon, the bear should already be aware he was around unless he was pretty far away. The comments from the guys back in the pub suggested that wasn't true.

He went to his site and took a few minutes to comb the ground and make sure no rocks, pinecones, or anything that would make an uncomfortable bed was present where he would set up his tent.

It didn't take him long to erect it and stow his gear inside. Ecaterina had gotten her personal tent up under the other trees and returned to the clearing, where she was starting a fire in the pit.

Fortunately, she was burning oak and not pine. He had seen a few of those on their trip up here, so that wasn't too surprising. He much preferred the smell of burning oak to pine.

He grabbed a metal backpackers' coffee pot and filled the filter with the ground coffee he had brought. After adding the water, he went over to the fire and handed it to Ecaterina. She set it to the side, for now. She would wait until she had more coals before nestling it down into them to make coffee.

There were beautiful sounds in the night: the owls, the wind, the occasional howl in the distance, and the crisp crackle and spitting of the wood as it burned.

He wasn't sure how long it would take before he was checked on, but he decided being asleep when it happened wasn't the way to make a good first impression.

They both enjoyed the night, the fire, and the smell of the freshly brewed coffee. They didn't speak much, just passed the time in companionable silence until Ecaterina wished him a good night, saying she would see him in the morning.

He had kept his eyes away from the fire so he wasn't blind when he stared into the dark. When Ecaterina went to her tent, he noted that she was very careful where she put her feet. He took a sip of his coffee and added a mental flag to the map that read, "here be traps."

After another hour, he decided to hit the sack himself. His eyes flicked to Ecaterina's tent, but he was old enough and had been through enough relationships to avoid the stupidity of approaching someone with her skills at night, no matter how interesting she was.

He got into his tent and laid on top of the sleeping bag, then let his senses roam and listened to the night. He would sleep very lightly tonight. Plus, he had gone around the campsite an hour before and dropped his sensors. That would give him about a hundred yards of electronic awareness, and anything outside he should sense.

He could hear her soft breathing across the clearing.

Bethany Anne was enjoying her descent when the wind, which had been wafting up the mountain as she came down, brought new scents she couldn't interpret.

She knew enough about humans both male and female to pick those out, but there was more to this than she had experienced so far.

She had smelled two humans, a male and female, much earlier in the day, and a little later two more males. Now she was picking up an animal of some kind. The problem was that none of the males had smelled completely human to her, and the animal shared the scent with the three males.

"TOM, do you have any idea what might smell like a male human but not really human? I'm sensing something like that."

No. I understand the difference, but if it were a change we had initiated, I would be able to tell since they have certain olfactory characteristics when they consume blood and perspire the poisons back out of their bodies. I am not familiar with the nuances you are smelling.

"Could it be one of the other Five, or God forbid, the Seven making changes here?"

She could tell he was thinking, and since she had a headache coming on, he must be accessing the computer. "You're giving me a headache. Give it your best shot without calculating it to perfection, all right?"

Sorry, it was a good question, and I didn't stop to think about it affecting you. While it is within the realm of possibility that the unknown humans are related to the Kurtherians, I don't think it has a high probability.

"Un-fucking-believable. I don't just have *your* race screwing us around, but now I have another race of modified humans and some other interstellar busybodies doing God-knows-what to deal with. Michael completely failed to give me the appropriate updates—or *I* didn't think to ask what else was out there, and it slipped his and Carl's mind. Either way, are they aware of the vamps? If they are, are they friends or foes, and will they attack as soon as they know I'm Michael's?"

Well, it would be difficult for them to say you are "Michael's" since he wasn't responsible for turning you. I was. And you haven't drunk any blood recently, so you don't have the vamp scent on you. It's daytime, and you're not affected, unlike most of Michael's children. I'm not sure they will have any idea you aren't human.

"Oh, is that so? Goody! Let's invite ourselves to this little party —although I'd rather stay away from the animal if that's possible.

Stick or no stick, I hate being a raging bitch when they're just acting as God intended. Well, considering the scent, maybe a bit more than God intended."

She picked up her pace, deciding it might be fun and informative to see what it felt like to jump twenty feet from boulder to boulder on her descent. At one point, she landed on some gravel and her foot slipped off. Her adrenaline kicked in and, dropping the stick, she spun on her axis in the air to face-down. Shoving hard with both hands off the boulder, she flipped backward to land in a crouch below the boulder.

A little shaken by her automatic reactions, she thought for a second about how fast it had happened. She picked up a stick and held it as high as her head, then dropped it and watched it hit the ground. The second time she flipped it a foot in the air and switched into high gear. Now the stick seemed to float lazily down, allowing her to reach out and snag the tip with two fingers before it fell a quarter of an inch. When she dropped back into normal speed, her perceptions were heightened, but not so much that everything seemed to be in super-slow motion like it had been a second ago.

Leaving the stick and picking up her staff, all she thought was *hmmm* as she started the ground-eating jumps again in the direction of the lake. She slowed down about a mile away, deciding to remain at that distance and approach in the morning. There wasn't a good reason to rush it, and arriving at night just freaked people—and potentially non-people—right the hell out.

That night she experimented with her speed to understand it better. TOM had assured her it didn't expend too much energy, which was a concern since she was still increasing her reserves after her meltdown the other day.

She used her senses to take in all the wildlife and noises she could hear. It became obvious the animals knew about *her* since the area went quiet when she came through.

She decided she must give off some sort of dangerous vibe the animals picked up on.

It was a couple of hours past dawn when she headed toward the people. She could hear talking from that direction, and smell the smoke.

Then she heard the gunshot.

CHAPTER EIGHTEEN

Carpathian Mountains, Romania

"*Gott Verdammt*, that hurts like a motherfucker!" Nathan had been getting up to get another cup of coffee from the pot Ecaterina had set up before breakfast when a bullet ripped through his shoulder, flipping him around and onto his back on the ground before the report from the gun reached him.

The shooter had to be at least a few hundred yards away for him not to have sensed them, and for the bullet to have reached him so far ahead of the sound.

If he hadn't been bending down to get another cup of coffee, that might have been a headshot. While he healed well, headshots were a dicey proposition—you might or might not come back with your brain screwed back in correctly.

Instead of the wound healing, it continued to hurt horribly, which meant they had used silver in the frangible. That was going to be a cold-blooded bitch to get out. Well, at least it let him know he was up against other Weres. No one else in their right mind would use silver in a bullet, because it was expensive and a truly poor substitute for other alloys, as well as being a right pain to fabricate.

Ecaterina had dropped her plate and shinnied over to her tent to grab her rifle, then slid behind one of the trees facing the direction the shot had come from.

Nathan didn't stay still. He was fighting the desire to change. The pain from the silver was incredible, but he had endured much worse in the war. He was trying to keep his anger tamped down. He didn't want to lose Ecaterina. If these idiots showed up as wolves, that was going to tear it. She was going to have to be wiped or something else horrible, and he really didn't want to go down that path. He hadn't known her long, but it felt like he had loved her spirit for ages. Those who love the outdoors and breathe it as the life-giving essence it is were rare. He didn't want to lose this chance with her—if he even had one.

But he needed to keep her alive to get that chance, and he hadn't brought a gun up here. He hadn't expected to be tailed by wolves on a bear's mountain. That was not wise , and nothing he had seen so far had suggested this team were idiots.

Until now.

He grabbed his Bowie from the tent. It had some silver in the blade, but not enough to truly harm a Were. That was why he had ten silver stakes with barbs. They went in easily, but if you tried to pull them out, you made a hell of a large, painful, and not-easily-healable mess.

Kind of like frangible silver bullets.

He wouldn't cry any tears over their pain.

He checked Ecaterina. She had almost vanished into the underbrush, which was incredibly good for a human, but she didn't realize she wasn't fighting humans. He could smell her from where he was.

Taking off his coat left him in a blood-soaked long-sleeved shirt, which was better than staying in his coat while trying to be quiet out there. He started in the direction of the gunshot.

He assumed these guys—he didn't smell a female—were from the local pack. He picked up three distinct scents.

He stopped to listen, and it became obvious that something was coming at him at speed from his left—something running on four legs.

Stupid fucking youngsters, he thought. *Well, I don't have the option of giving this one a chance to learn.*

Nathan moved to the right of a large pine, putting the tree between him and the oncoming Were.

Thinking to surprise him, the growling Were dodged around the tree and leaped at his throat, teeth bared, ready to bring him down.

Nathan calmly swung his right fist—the one holding the knife—toward the wolf's neck as he dodged it by ducking under its jump. Yelping in pain from the silver and the massive hole in its neck, it lost the focus to land properly and broke its right foreleg.

Rushing over before it could move, Nathan grabbed the muzzle and the back of the head and gave a guttural grunt as he twisted it quickly, snapping the vertebra. The wolf, who was only a young adult, stopped moving.

Nathan pulled his knife out, made the sign of the cross over the body, and drifted into the woods again.

A sudden scream got his attention, and a second later a male voice came from the camp. "Lowell, we have the girl. We can end this quickly, or we can take our time. You're not getting off this mountain. Sorry to say you picked a bad side to join, my friend."

Nathan was pissed. He was supposed to leave Ecaterina behind; he had an operation to focus on. The chances of her surviving this situation were becoming infinitesimally small. If he died, she would too. If he lived but showed the UnknownWorld to her and she talked, she was signing her own death certificate. It was highly unlikely he could take out both—no, he could sense three now—other Weres without her getting hurt in the process.

What did the SWAT teams back at home say about this? Oh, yeah: "It sucks to be the hostage."

The Weres, however, had attacked them both, and for that, they were going to die. The only question was how soon. They would have to kill him to stop him, and since they had obviously planned on that, it became a choice between them and him. He always bet on himself, but how to help Ecaterina?

As he was circling back around the campsite, he heard one of the Weres yell, "Bitch!" then a smack and a thump as a body hit the ground.

Then, "Nathan, I can't say she will die quickly and cleanly— can't let that attack go. But now she's going to have to wake up. What do you say...you want this quick, or shall we draw it out? I would enjoy hurting her slowly."

Good for you, Ecaterina, thought Nathan. She wouldn't take any shit from anybody. He wasn't sure how they had caught her, but Weres in their natural habitat, whether as humans or wolves, could almost ghost across the ground.

He could see into the clearing. Ecaterina was draped across a log near the fire. She must have been sitting down and bitten a hand holding her there. Slapping her had knocked her out, but he couldn't see her face on the other side of the log.

They wanted him to come into the clearing, back where their sniper would have another shot.

That wasn't going to work, not unless he darted in as a wolf.

That was when the roaring started.

Alexi was pissed. He had strolled in a leisurely fashion from his den to the clearing where Ecaterina had bedded down, and then he went fishing in the lake. He enjoyed the fish on the south side the most, and he had decided there was no reason to talk to them that evening. He would go tomorrow morning and have his discussion with the fucking new guy.

As he was coming up from the lake, he heard the gunshot and got his ponderous body moving toward Ecaterina's location. He achieved both a full run and a righteous and bloody anger, driven partly by fear of what he might find.

Ecaterina wouldn't take a shot unless something was stalking her, and he doubted she had allowed her customer to bring a rifle. This meant someone was hunting, and they were very near his niece.

He could smell the Weres; they were from the Brasov pack. They had dared to come onto his mountain and hunt? This was too much. He roared in anger, and he roared his announcement that there would be no capitulation. When he thundered into the clearing, he saw Ecaterina's body draped over a log near the fire and one of the pack working his hand.

The tall Were, his huge chest covered by a red shirt, turned to face Alexi as the first bullet ripped into the bear's shoulder, causing him to stagger to the right. He grew angrier, the pain from the wound paling against the prospect of getting his teeth into the animal in front of him.

The second bullet tore into his back left leg and he stumbled again and rolled, then he shook his head and roared his response to the pack's cheap tricks. They were not even honorable enough to face him in combat but shot him from afar.

The pack member roared with laughter as he gazed at Alexi, knowing the next shot would kill him since Alexi couldn't move as quickly now.

They heard the report, but nothing raced down to end Alexi's life. The pack member was looking over his left shoulder across a small valley when a huge black blur raced from his opposite side and bowled him over. They both left the clearing, crashing through the bushes and trees.

Alexi stood up and took several painful steps over to Ecaterina's body. She was breathing but had a horrible bloody gash above her right eye. Alexi roared his anger that anything should have hurt his niece. He landed back on his feet, blood coming from his shoulder and his leg. They'd lost their sniper, so nothing else would happen to his niece. If they hadn't, he would already have been dead.

CHAPTER NINETEEN

Carpathian Mountains, Romania

The bear occupied the focus of the Were near Ecaterina. Nathan stripped out of his clothes. Taking the Bowie and a stick from the ground, he bit down on the stick and used the Bowie to dig the silver bits out of his shoulder. The pain from the silver in the Bowie was horrendous, but the desire to protect the woman steadied his hand as he worked the bullet's pieces out. Sweat beaded his forehead.

He heard a gunshot.

He set the knife down and used his fingers to dig into his shoulder and grab the last piece, and threw it down in disgust. The silver was out and his natural healing was already working, so now he could focus enough to change.

One second a naked man with blood dripping from his shoulder stood there, and the next it was a black wolf with green human-like eyes. Wasting no time, the wolf took off at speed as it heard a second shot and laughter from the clearing.

Focused on both speed and stealth, Nathan took too long to get back to the clearing. He heard a third shot.

Coming through the trees from behind his tent, he saw a man

looking in the other direction. The bear was in obvious pain, but was starting to get back up and had eyes only for the guy by the fire.

Tough shit. This asshole was *his*, so he hit him going as fast as he could run. He gripped the asshole's shoulder in his teeth, and they tumbled into the bushes.

A little shaken up, it took Nathan a few seconds to get his bearings and ascertain where his adversary had ended up. The guy was about twenty feet away, and had just stripped and finished his change.

Nathan was huge for a natural wolf, and even for a Were he was a spectacular size, but this guy had him beat by twenty pounds at least. Dusk-colored, his black eyes bore almost no intelligence beyond animal cunning. Growling, the two wolves circled each other, looking for an opening.

His opponent barked. There was an answering bark from the campsite, and Nathan heard another wolf coming toward them.

Great, it was going to be two on one. *Fine.* That left one for the bear, so he couldn't complain later that Nathan had taken the easy way out.

The other wolf came into the clearing, and Nathan had to work to keep them in front of him. If either one of them came in and grabbed a back leg in their teeth, his day was going to go into the shitter for sure.

The gunshot came from ahead and to her left.

She started running, but this time it was different. She was in her zone now; every leaf, every branch was in complete detail as she chose exactly where to place each foot or hand as she jumped over fallen trees or dodged between standing ones or used branches as shortcuts through the dense foliage.

Dimly she heard a roar, although the sound took forever to

MICHAEL ANDERLE

reach her as she moved. What she could, she ran over. What she couldn't, she ran through or across. Nothing would stop her from finding the shooter.

She spotted the weapon, then the sniper.

She jumped from her location to the first wall and started pulling herself up. There was nothing too tiny for her to use as leverage to climb. He was more than a hundred feet above her...seventy feet...forty feet.

He fired again. She moved across the face of the cliff trying to find a handhold...*any* handhold.

In frustration she drove her fist into the stone, aggregate shooting from the resulting hole.

He was lining up for another shot. She wouldn't be in time. Determination fueled her anxiety as frustration pierced her anger.

The world flashed white, and suddenly she was falling toward him from above. She punched the back of his head, and his finger pulled the trigger as she came crashing down into his body. His head, however, had already hit the stock and shoved the barrel upward. The shot wouldn't strike anyone down in the valley.

And he wouldn't ever shoot anyone again. His head had just about exploded from her punch. His blood was all over her hand.

We are down to almost nothing on our energy reserves.

"What the hell just happened?" Bethany Anne struggled off the corpse and grabbed the sniper rifle to use the scope to see what was going on down in the valley.

You transported your body above the victim, and, well, you know the rest.

"Yeah, but how did I do it?" A wounded bear was protecting a woman from two rather large wolves, then one took off into the bushes. This left one harassing the bear.

"How much would it take to transport down there?" Bethany Anne pointed to the clearing, which was at least a thousand feet from where they presently were.

Too much. You would need a significant Etheric balance to

164

make that jump. We will become more efficient at using your reserves with every jump, but right now you don't have it, and you won't for some time...well before that is finished.

"How much blood?"

Excuse me?

"How much blood would I have to consume to get the energy I need? She needs me." The anger was starting to show in Bethany Anne's eyes. Her hatred of the strong preying on the week, her fury at what was right getting lost to what bad people forced on others. This wasn't happening to her or to that woman down below.

Bethany Anne decided she was going to become that which the monsters feared. If they feared Michael because of his honor, they were going to fear Bethany Anne because hell hath no fury like a woman protecting her own. And the defenseless were indeed Bethany Anne's own. There was nothing in life, or death, that would stop her.

Well, I truly couldn't say. We would need to try a little, and then I could—

"Tell me when I've got enough." With that Bethany Anne grabbed the body with her right hand, never taking her eyes from the clearing below. She lifted the two-hundred-pound corpse as if it weighed the same as a sack of potatoes, and started sucking blood from the neck with incisors that grew as her eyes became red. Then she disappeared, and the corpse fell back to the ground with a sickening plop.

The second wolf took off into the bushes, and Alexi could hear the growling. It had just become a two-against-one battle.

That left him the one, and this wolf wasn't stupid. Every time Alexi tried to get a good position the wolf would jump toward Ecaterina, causing Alexi to have to come back and swat the wolf away to protect her. He was unable to defend her proactively.

Then life suddenly got very weird.

Alexi was almost standing over Ecaterina. He was staring at the wolf, who was obviously trying to decide the best way to get to the girl, when a woman appeared from thin air behind the wolf. She had blood all over her mouth and right hand and picked the Were up with her left, then slapped it with her right. The wolf's head disintegrated, and she dropped its body and walked into the bushes toward the fight.

Oh, this is bad, thought Alexi. He could smell what this being was, and while he hadn't been around one in many years, you never forgot the smell of a vampire—or the destruction they could bring.

Well, if he died protecting Ecaterina, it wouldn't be a mangy wolf he lost his life to. He moved to stand between the bushes and his precious niece, ready to take on Death herself to give Ecaterina one more chance at life.

CHAPTER TWENTY

<u>Carpathian Mountains, Romania</u>

Nathan was in a real quandary. The new wolf was moving into position, so he was going to have to make the decision to stay here or see if he could join up with the bear and make it a two-against-three fight. Hopefully, the big guy would recognize him, not just knock him ass over appetite the first chance he got.

Bears were notorious for being loners. They didn't form groups as animals, and werebears weren't much different.

All three of the wolves in the bushes heard a sudden loud and meaty whack from the clearing, and the wolf out there was suddenly quiet. A body hit the ground.

The bear moved a little toward them...and then all three wolves heard the footsteps.

Slow, distinctly human footsteps.

There was only one human out here, but Nathan didn't think she was stupid enough to come into the bushes when three wolves were fighting.

A human female materialized in front of them and looked at all three. Their fight was put on hold until this new situation could be assessed.

MICHAEL ANDERLE

Oh, holy shit, thought Nathan. If the blood on her hands and throat and staining her mouth didn't give it away, the freaking blood-red eyes were a big sign he'd found the new family member.

Apparently, she didn't need Michael holding her hand—and she was walking in the daytime.

Well, fuckity fuck. This had gone from bad to worse. If she was going to ask questions of the dead, then Nathan was officially a goner.

He had hopes she was at least neutral since he could still hear the bear near Ecaterina.

Then the newest wolf decided to end his participation in the truce by attacking her. Death by vampire was usually quick, at least in Nathan's experience, and this wasn't any different.

The wolf, who weighed at least eighty pounds, leaped at the vampire. She continued to watch both him and the other Alpha as she casually grabbed the jumping werewolf by the throat, stopping his leap in midair, then ripped his head back, snapping his neck and spraying the area with his arterial blood. She calmly put the body to her mouth while keeping her blood-red eyes on the other two as she sucked down the freshly-killed wolf's essence. Dropping the body at her feet, she stepped over it and quietly ordered, "Change back to your human forms or die. I won't give you a third option."

Nathan laid down to change back into a human, and the other wolf seized the opportunity to try to bury his teeth in Nathan's neck.

He didn't make it to Nathan. The vampire was ten feet away one second, and the next had the Alpha slammed into the dirt near Nathan—who was now fully human and naked.

She cocked her head as if thinking, then casually used her forearm to crack the other Alpha over the head; not killing him, but rather knocking him unconscious.

She lifted the Alpha by the scruff of the neck like a puppy and walked toward the clearing, saying, "Get dressed and meet me by the woman."

There was a reason Gerry always had Nathan communicate and liaise with Michael and his family. It was because he never *ever* got stupid around vampires.

***

Alexi heard a short bark of surprise and flesh ripping, then blood pumping. A moment later a body hit the ground, and the vampire gave the other two an ultimatum.

Alexi didn't have time to wonder if either would be stupid before he heard a body slam into the ground and a meaty smack, and the vampire moving in his direction while telling the last wolf to get dressed.

She appeared in the clearing with fresh blood around her mouth and down her throat. It didn't seem like it bothered her too much. She carried the Alpha like a pup and casually threw him down at Alexi's feet.

"Don't let him go. Sit on him if you have to. I want answers, and he's going to give them to me. I'll be back."

With that announcement, she disappeared toward the lake.

Alexi looked down at the wolf and considered just ending its life, but he decided he didn't want to press a daywalking vampire's patience right off the bat.

The silver was beginning to really annoy him as the other guy, the one Ecaterina had brought up here, came out of the bushes. He walked past Alexi, giving him a nod of respect, and went over to his tent. He reached in and pulled out a bag. Getting out a change of clothes, he brushed off the dirt on his skin and got dressed. Then he took a first aid kit from his backpack. Walking over to Alexi and Ecaterina, he held out the kit.

"Do you mind if I clean up the wound? I don't think it will go away by itself, and she can't be comfortable in that position. You can keep an eye on large and stupid here better than I can. I don't want to be in wolf form when dark, bloody, and freaking dangerous comes back."

Alexi rested a dinner-plate-sized paw on top of the sleeping Alpha.

Nathan gently pulled Ecaterina off the log and laid her out carefully on the ground. Opening the first aid kit, he pulled out the antiseptic wipes and started cleaning her wound.

By the time he was finished, the vampire was back. She had washed as well as she could in the lake. She obviously didn't care if they wanted her there.

The vampire was stunning if you liked your ladies with dark hair and destructive urges. She came up to Nathan and Ecaterina after sparing a glance at the bear holding down the wolf.

"How is she doing?"

Her voice was soft, which was completely different from earlier. Then her voice had been death, just slightly warmer.

Nathan took a moment to respond, carefully weighing his words. "I think she'll do okay. These types of wounds on humans can keep them out for a long time. I think she'll be awake before sunset. Look, I don't think she understands anything about the UnknownWorld, so I hope you don't feel a need to wipe her."

Alexi would have held his breath if he were in human form. For Nathan to be forward enough to suggest a vampire go against Michael's law of keeping humans as ignorant as possible regarding the UnknownWorld was chancy, and gave Alexi a little insight into Nathan's thoughts about his niece.

That was when the wolf started coming around.

Bethany Anne checked on the woman in the werewolf's arms. He was obviously taking care of her, so she didn't feel uncomfortable leaving the woman with him.

His question was a little off-putting. Would she *wipe* her? Obviously, that was some kind of rule or suggestion or something about the UnknownWorld. She had heard the "UnknownWorld" term used a couple of times, but not in the context of werewolves and werebears—or maybe she should just say Weres and leave it at that? No matter; she wasn't wiping anybody.

It was an easy decision; people shouldn't have chunks of their lives wiped clean. She didn't know how to wipe anyone anyway. Although she could ask TOM, better to be ignorant if she talked with Michael.

The wolf was starting to move and fidget. She stood up and walked over to him so she would be visible when he opened his eyes.

She listened to the heartbeat and the breathing and enjoyed the fact the wolf was trying to pretend he was still unconscious. Trying to heal, she surmised.

Unworried, she walked over to the fire and selected a small partially-unburned limb. She casually pulled it free of the fire and told the bear, "You'll want to hold him still for this," then flung the limb onto the wolf's flank.

That woke him right the hell up. The wolf was promising violence with his growling and barking; too bad for him that he couldn't move worth a damn with more than a thousand pounds of bear holding him down.

Bethany Anne walked back over to the wolf, who followed her with his eyes and slowly stopped his useless struggling.

"You have two options. You can change back, or I can continue to cause you pain until you die. If you try to hold out on me, I'm going to get my pound of flesh from you whether you choose to give up early or late. So, what's it going to be?"

The wolf looked like he wanted to bite her, but a second later, there was a naked man under the bear's paw.

Bethany Anne looked at the man holding the girl. "You got anything for him you don't mind losing?"

He returned her gaze, a little confused, but then dipped his head toward a tent. "Back in my tent, black bag. There's another pair of pants and a shirt."

Bethany Anne walked over to the tent, dug out the bag, and grabbed the clothes. When she got back to the Were, she flung them at his feet. "Put those on. I don't want the condemned to be naked."

The guy acted affronted. "Condemned? I've not done anything wrong. That man is in our territory without permission! I'm just protecting my homeland. Stephen has allowed us to protect our territory for the past four centuries. That is how it has always been." The bear had released him to let him dress.

Stephen was Michael's child, and he lived somewhere near here. Towards the water, if she remembered correctly. Not that she cared a whit what Stephen thought. If he could allow a travesty such as this to occur, he would be getting a visit from her soon enough. If he wasn't awake, well, she would wake him the hell up by putting him in the sun until he chose to open his eyes, then they would be able to talk like sensible supernatural adults—right before she kicked his ass for being a careless twit—unless Stephen was the one who could walk in the sun as well. She couldn't remember if that was Stephen or David. Either way, they would have a discussion after a proper introduction.

"You have a name?" Bethany Anne chose to sit down on a log. It helped the guy feel more comfortable, since he was standing up and in a higher position. It allowed her to set up a perfect and rational demonstration.

"I am the Alpha of the Brasov Pack, and my name is Algerian. You and these trespassers need to get off our land before I speak with Stephen and he speaks with Michael."

This guy wanted to eat his own leg, apparently.

Calmly, Bethany Anne started the object lesson. "Algerian, you need to sit down."

"I'll do no such—" He landed on his ass before he could finish the sentence, and Bethany Anne was back on the log like she had never moved.

"Good of you to sit. If you choose to get up, I'll find a few branches to impale you with until you stay down. Do you understand the conditions, Algerian?"

He nodded his head sullenly.

She looked at the bear. "You need to get that silver out. I can smell the reaction with your flesh. Come here."

CHAPTER TWENTY-ONE

Carpathian Mountains, Romania

Alexi was startled. He had stayed mostly out of the limelight because of the wolf's antics.

Now she was looking at him. Part of him was still put out that this had gone down on his mountain. He had been lord of this domain for the last thirty or more years, only to have been brought close to death because of the silver in the bullets from what he had thought was a powerless pack. Now he was taking orders from a woman who couldn't weigh much more than a hundred and thirty pounds, although she was taller than average for a female.

Considering that the silver was hurting, he decided going along would be a good choice.

He walked toward the vampire, who had stood up. He considered taking a bite out of Algerian on his way past, but he consoled himself with the thought that werewolves probably didn't taste very good.

She came around to his injured side and looked at the wounds. She cocked her head and seemed to go inside herself for a few seconds before placing her left hand on his back and looking him straight in the eyes. "You ready for a little pain? Because, if you bite me, I'm going to make you regrow a whole arm instead of the little bit of meat that's going to come out with the bullets. You understand?"

Alexi nodded in agreement. While he wouldn't have believed it when he was on his way over this morning, he knew now that if this woman said she would pull his arm off, he would be losing it. Well, he thought, she wasn't *that* small for a human, but in his bear form, she seemed tiny.

The pain was sudden, it was sharp, it was excruciating, and then it was over. She had jumped into super-speed, reached into his wounds, found the pieces, and pulled them all out. He carefully kept his legs locked as he roared his pain.

"Give it a rest, you big brown baby. Now change."

Alexi lay down on the ground, his side slowly mending. His desire to turn his head and bite her was fortunately overwhelmed by his desire not to get his ass kicked by a girl. In a second, he was naked.

"God, a year ago I couldn't find a good man, and now there are all kinds of hunky guys lying around naked. Go find something to cover yourself with. Ask your lady friend if you need to; she's awake." She walked over to Algerian.

He glanced at Ecaterina. The man who was holding her was looking down in surprise. He had been watching what was going on with the vampire and hadn't noticed her waking up in his arms.

Ecaterina was in someone's arms and her head was pounding, but the pain was manageable.

Last she remembered, she was being held down by the guy over there in the jeans that looked a little too small on him. There was a woman next to the biggest brown bear she had ever seen;

her eyes widened. She was talking to the bear, and then suddenly it just appeared to become less solid. The bear roared in pain, but its legs stayed still.

The woman talked to the bear as if it could understand her. Ecaterina watched in fascination as it laid down, and then a naked man was in its place.

Her breath caught in her throat. The woman told the bear-man to find some clothes because she was awake.

Nathan jerked, and she could tell she was now the focus of both the bear-man and Nathan.

The man with no clothes was familiar. "Uncle Alexi?"

She must have really taken a knock on the head. Her uncle was rarely in town. He was a favorite of hers, but she hadn't seen him in…what, eight years?

"Yeah, it's me, Ecaterina. Do you happen to have anything I could wear?"

Nathan, his voice above her, spoke instead. "Hey, I've got the pants I had on earlier this morning. They might be a little big, but they're about a hundred meters away. If you want to, go get them."

The woman glanced at Nathan. "Which direction?"

Nathan took an arm from around Ecaterina and pointed behind his tent. "Back that way. There's a ravine about forty yards in. There's a dead wolf. The clothes will be about thirty yards downhill from there."

The woman was gone. The man, Algerian, came out of his lethargy and jumped up and started in Ecaterina's direction. Ecaterina could feel Nathan tense and get ready to do something when Algerian seemed to fly back to his original location with a big Bowie knife through his hand, pinning it to the dirt. He screamed in pain. The lady appeared at his side and pushed the knife farther into his palm, ignoring his useless efforts to pull it out.

She tossed the clothes to Ecaterina's uncle, who stood up to put them on. Ecaterina averted her eyes.

She looked down at Algerian. "You don't learn very quickly, do you? I explained what I was going to do. If you don't remember, or you decide you have more important things to do, I will provide an object lesson to keep you focused. Now, I *had* promised you tree limbs, but I really liked the Bowie knife. So, let's keep this right where it is, or I'll find a five-inch sapling to use as my next stake. Do you understand me, Algerian?"

Her voice was calm, as if she were discussing the fact that they might get a little shower later in the afternoon.

The man was sweating now, despite how cool it was, and his hand was swelling up.

As she walked over to them, Nathan's arms tensed around Ecaterina. He seemed to know something about this woman and certainly seemed concerned for Ecaterina's safety. So far, she wasn't sure why. Well, except for the whole disappearing, stronger-than-she-should-be, speaking-softly-as-she-pinned-people's-hands-to-the-dirt-with-a-knife part.

Yeah, maybe this knock on Ecaterina's head wasn't allowing her to think clearly. She should be terrified.

Ecaterina looked up into the woman's eyes, which seemed soft and caring. The woman took a knee in front of Ecaterina. "My name is Bethany Anne. How are you feeling?"

Ecaterina's voice was a little weaker than normal, but she answered her question. "Fine, mostly. My head hurts, and I'm confused. Why is my uncle a bear? Why is there a knife through that guy's hand, and why is there a wolf with a missing head over there?" Ecaterina raised her chin in the direction of the wolf's body and was reminded that sudden movements caused unreasonable pain. She closed her eyes.

Bethany Anne looked where Ecaterina was trying to point and

turned back to face her. "Well, to tell you the truth, he's a werewolf like our friend Algerian over there."

Ecaterina could feel Nathan tense again, a motion that wasn't lost on Bethany Anne. "Is there a problem with me explaining that to Ecaterina? You know, I never got your name."

"Nathan. Nathan Lowell."

"Ah, a fellow American. So, care to share why you're so tense?"

"It's, ah…" Nathan dragged the word out searching for a tactful way to say it wasn't a normal vampire command.

"Mr. Lowell, I'm not very politically correct amongst the vampires. In fact, I think you'll find I've had about as much bullshit from Michael as I care to take, and since he left me to clean up his mess—my words, not his—I don't have any rats' asses left to give about what any of the rest of his children think."

Nathan seemed to be completely befuddled by Bethany Anne's statement. His jaw opened and shut at least three times.

Hell, she was taking it better than Nathan, even that her uncle was a werebear. Why was he upset with the woman about some guy named Michael?

Nathan seemed to get it together on the fourth try. "It's standard procedure, dictated by Michael and enforced by all of his children, that any human encountering the UnknownWorld will have their mind wiped. You're saying that you won't do that?"

Bethany Anne stood up, walked over to Algerian, and pulled the knife out of his hand. He grabbed it to slow the bleeding. Bethany Anne calmly reached down and wiped the knife clean on his jeans.

"Mr. Lowell, it sounds like you are someone I want to talk to. Someone who has a more intimate knowledge of how things worked around our little ball of sunshine before Michael decided to change the tune." She turned back to look down at Algerian again and continued, "However, to answer your question, no, I am not going to do that. I doubt a woman of Ecaterina's caliber is a problem for me.

"Algerian, why did you really try to kill my good friend Nathan over here?" She waved the Bowie knife, catching his attention. Without saying it, she was suggesting that anything less than the truth would probably end in something painful.

"I was told to do it."

She got down and stared at him at eye level. "By whom, Algerian?" Her voice was silk over the steel. Ecaterina wanted to answer the question. She felt *compelled* to answer the question, but she didn't have a clue what they were talking about.

"Petre."

"Who is Petre, Algerian?"

"He is Stephen's second son, and he is responsible for this territory. He will help protect us from Stephen if he wakes up."

"So, Stephen doesn't know Petre is encouraging your pack to behave this way?"

"No."

"And did you have a legitimate concern with Mr. Lowell being here?"

"No. He called and got permission to visit. Petre was in our offices when it happened and told us to approve the request. Petre thought he was searching for Michael and his new child candidate."

"Do you know why that would be important to Petre, Algerian?"

"They are vampires, so it is always best not to be too curious."

"Hmmm, good to know that's a universal consensus, although it speaks to a general feeling of a group known for being bullies if you ask me...which you didn't."

Bethany Anne stood up, turned to Alexi, and cocked her head. "Do you have any questions you want answered?"

Alexi answered, "Not from him, but if I can be so bold, one from you?"

"If I can answer it, sure."

"What are your plans for Algerian?"

"He was condemned by his actions in the fight earlier. He was told to change back to human or die, and he chose death by trying to strike down Mr. Lowell here."

"Do you need to be the executioner?"

Bethany Anne thought about that for a moment. Did she? It had been her word that he would die if he failed to follow her commands, but did she need to carry it out personally or would it be okay if she just confirmed it was accomplished?

"Do you have an outstanding issue with him?"

"He came on my land and attacked and hurt my family, his pack shot me twice, and if you hadn't interfered, I would probably be dead right now. But if you mean before today, then no."

"Well, you getting shot happened before he ignored my command, so I'm okay if you want to claim precedence on retribution. But he must die now, or I will take care of it."

Alexi started getting undressed again, and Bethany Anne turned back around to the man who seemed not to be listening to anything going on around him. "Algerian."

"Yes."

"I want you to prepare for combat in the bushes where I found you. When you hear a bear's roar, change back into your wolf form. You may fight until your dying breath. Do you understand my command?"

"Yes."

"Make it happen. You have provided me with the information, which stayed my hand earlier."

Alexi finished undressing. One second, he was a man, the next he was a huge brown bear again. He walked calmly into the bushes in front of Ecaterina, and the other man followed him.

A minute later there was a roar that shook Ecaterina's insides and then the horrible sounds of a wolf and a bear fighting. There was a sudden sharp bark and a loud thump as a body hit a tree and slid down. Two more loud noises, then the bushes were brushed aside and a large body came back into the clearing.

Alexi had a few scratches, but he didn't seem too concerned.

Bethany Anne looked at him. "Alexi, I'll watch Ecaterina through the night, and we'll leave for Brasov in the morning. I expect you to join us. You are free to make whatever preparations are necessary for a week's absence. Make sure you dress comfortably. Not that it matters, but I completely approve of your reasons for taking Algerian down. All it takes is good men looking the other way to allow evil to get a foothold in our world."

She turned toward Ecaterina and Lowell. "I'll be back in another hour or so. There are a few things I want to retrieve, and then we can talk." She looked down at Ecaterina. "Are you feeling okay?"

"I am, thank you. I could use some aspirin and food right now, and although Mr. Lowell is quite warm, I think I would like to change clothes and freshen up a little."

"Very good. I'll see you both soon."

And with that, she walked out of the clearing.

CHAPTER TWENTY-TWO

Carpathian Mountains, Romania

Bethany Anne left the party in the clearing and quickly gained some distance from them, running around the north side of the lake. She wasn't sure how sensitive the Were-humans were, but she didn't want them to see any weakness from her—and right now she felt incredibly weak as she disgorged everything from her stomach. The disgusting regurgitation, along with the smell, caused her stomach another round of convulsions. She ran another fifty yards or so after each episode to get away from the smell.

TOM was trying to say something, but she couldn't listen right then. Mentally, she was prepared to do anything—including eating people, whether human or wolf at the time—to acquire the energy she needed to protect Ecaterina and Alexi.

Until she had enough energy to be in top form, she could allow nothing to come between her and her need to protect them. That included being completely grossed out by her own actions. She turned off that part of her mind and took almost an analytical perspective.

The payment, in this case, was throwing up over parts of Alexi's mountain. She hoped he didn't mind if he ever found out.

She found a little stream and cleaned her mouth and cheeks and sat for a moment to consider her next step.

Unfortunately the lack of information—due no doubt to making sure she didn't have too much information if her transfer went wrong—was a real problem right then.

Michael must never have considered just how different her conversion would be. Since he'd never had a conversation with TOM nor any frame of reference for what the spacecraft was when he had stumbled upon it, he must have originally thought it was voodoo or magic or something. He had never explained his thoughts to her.

But during the last hundred years, he must have reconsidered the truth of his origins and realized it wasn't necessarily an evil device. Since TOM had so horribly messed up the first transformation he had tried due to no communication and Michael's substantial pain, it was no surprise the patriarch hadn't brought anyone else to the ship.

It was a little curious how and why Michael could implement the change.

"TOM, how can Michael and his children create new vampires?" She let her senses roam while she sat there listening to the abnormally-quiet forest. She could sense the animals deciding she wasn't on the hunt. She wondered if they could sense her mood.

I speculate that if you exchange enough of the blood of a human with enough of Michael's or one he changed, the blood will become saturated enough with the nanocytes that facilitate the enhancements. A smaller amount would just enhance a human with intrinsic body abnormalities, but there wouldn't be enough to overcome their bio-programming and replicate to complete the transformation.

Bethany Anne pondered this information. "If we do a reverse transfusion, can we undo the Kurtherian change?"

No. The changes we implement in a human body, once saturation is achieved in the first place, eventually replace all essential cells. A blood transfusion would not exchange the cells that have replicated in the organs, especially the brain.

"What about for a new transfer?"

Possibly. If the nanocytes have followed the programming, it is possible to interrupt the transition if you reduce the saturation point before they make too many inroads into the inner organs.

"What is the programming you are referring to?"

Stage 1: The nanocytes heal the body of any injury. Stage 2: the nanocytes review any DNA-level issues, like your leg modifications. Once those changes are complete, Stage 3 begins: Integrate with all core body functionality. Once the core body changes are complete, there is no going back.

"What would happen if injury occurred during Stage Two?"

Well, we assumed a body would be in our ship during these changes, so we didn't necessarily consider what would happen. I would imagine all changes to the DNA would stop at a safe stage, and every effort would be made to resume taking care of the Stage One directives.

"Why are Michael's children less powerful, and each generation substantially more affected by sunlight?"

I would guess that the nanocytes are a little less pure when they move from one human to another. The nanocytes already have the DNA changes from the original host—changes from Michael to his first level offspring—so those children's nanocytes have *two* sets of DNA changes when they change a third level, and so on. I'm sure the purity of the DNA in a child would potentially help or hinder a transformation, as well as the purity of the nanocytes that they receive.

As for the sunlight issue, I can only conclude that each

generation must be exchanging the epidermal layer with confused nanocytes. It must have happened in Michael's skin, and although he isn't affected, it was a recessive trait that became dominant in most of his children.

"Yeah, he has one—David, I think—who isn't affected. I think he's the only one."

Bethany Anne went quiet for a couple of minutes, trying to digest everything. "TOM, why are you qualifying your statements so much?"

I'm not sure of the answers. I thought it was normal not to state something you didn't know as truth?

"No, it isn't. What I mean to ask is, you seem to be more unsure of your answers than I would have thought you would be, since you had responsibility for implementing the solutions."

Well, I am a pilot first and a scientist a somewhat distant second. In our race, the truly intellectual have an overdeveloped sense of curiosity with a substantially higher level of risk-aversion. To be willing to rush into the unknown, we had to find those with intelligence, but not so much that they realized their peril was a given. We had to have the ability to persuade ourselves to take a spaceship, alone, and go out into the universe without even a map.

Bethany Anne was surprised. She hadn't given TOM the respect he probably deserved. While she was still a little annoyed over the fact that she had become his taxi, she was put into the rare position of being able to make a difference in more than just a few cold cases. She now potentially had a thousand years or more to make a difference.

Thinking about her situation, she knew that getting information was her first priority. She was effectively safe, and she already had at least two sources of information and a third she was going to visit. While Petre wasn't an immediate child and therefore almost assuredly wasn't a physical match for Bethany

Anne—hell, maybe none of the children could match her in a fight —he wouldn't be unprotected.

Especially if he were dealing under the table against his father. The children might not support Michael's black-and-white version of the world, but she couldn't imagine they would countenance a child working with the disowned or other groups who actively participated in attacking anything of Michael's.

She supposed she could talk to Stephen first, but that wasn't her style. The UnknownWorld would certainly form their own opinions of her from the stories told about her. While she might change a few opinions, there was no way she would be able to get ahead of gossip. That was probably the only thing faster than the speed of light. She smiled at the thought.

She needed to find out what had happened to Michael; if he was dead or had been captured or was just AWOL. She frowned at that option. It would piss her off more to find out he had purposely left her behind than if he were dead. That wasn't a nice thought if she were to be honest with herself, but she had a heightened level of abandonment issues. Could be why she was a little aloof with personal relationships, since most guys in their twenties had their own issues about being dependable.

She also had the matter Michael was tracking down—the new type of vamps who were somehow connected with the situation during World War II. If Michael wasn't personally dealing with that, and at the moment she couldn't assume he was, she would have to handle it.

Plus, some group was actively trying to get rid of her. It was obvious from Algerian's story that Petre didn't want Nathan getting involved.

Without Carl, she was seriously hampered in information acquisition. She needed to find a core group who knew more about the UnknownWorld and could help her understand what she could and couldn't accomplish with the movers and shakers in that area. If Carl and Michael had both been taken out of the equation, she would need to build her own team. She had some people she could contact from her previous life, but that would be chancy as hell. They would have split allegiances; her friendship wasn't going to trump their fealty to the US.

Then she would need funding. Her previous Bethany Anne Reynolds finances had probably already been dispersed, especially after the going-away party she and her father put on her credit cards that last night. That might have been a little irresponsible in light of what had happened to her since, but it had been a hell of a night. She would have to see what was in the accounts Michael had had Carl set up for her.

Her father would certainly be on her side, but getting in touch with him would be a real problem. Whoever was after her would expect contact, so she would have to be careful before getting him involved. The same would be true for Martin if she could convince herself it would be safe to confide anything in him.

She stood up and moved her head from side to side, cracking her neck. It was time to get back and find out what resources she *did* have. As far as she knew she had a wolf, a bear, a pretty Romanian girl, and the name of someone who could supply information.

Well, she had wanted to be on the sharp end, and it didn't get any sharper than where she was. She considered her options and the number of challenges ahead. Oh well, no time like the present to get some more information and let Petre suffer for his sins.

She set off back toward the camp.

Nathan was sitting on a log next to what was now mostly just ashes in the firepit and tossed in a couple of small logs as he considered the situation.

Obviously, he had found Michael's new child, and she was nothing like he had expected. Well, mostly not.

She had the scary-as-hell-kill-you-dead part down pat. His wolf would normally have issues with challenges, but she was so far above him that the wolf just accepted her Alpha-ness. He only accepted Gerry as an Alpha because Gerry never pushed it. He asked Nathan to do something for him, and Nathan was as happy with the relationship as he possibly could be.

Until this little trip, working with Michael's group had been high-risk and low-probability, so he'd only had to keep his head down for a short time to come out ahead. The risk had been more than enough to keep him out of everything else related to the pack.

It seemed he had lost the roll of the dice now. If he ever got out of this situation, he would have to admit that Gerry had played the better long game. Nathan's markers had all come due, and the bill was going to be significantly higher than he thought he would ever have to pay. That tended to tip the scales to the "I'm so screwed" side.

However, Ecaterina was on the other side of the scale, so it was possible he would still come out ahead. One should always look for the sunshine peeking over the mountain in the morning. The view was breathtaking.

Speaking of breathtaking, Ecaterina was presently kneeling with her head inside her tent and the rest of her body outside, and the view was causing him serious problems. My God...

"What exactly has your attention, Mr. Lowell?"

His face got red. Nathan had forgotten about Ecaterina's uncle, who had finished cleaning up the bodies and dumped them away from their site. He quickly pulled his attention back to the flame and blurted out the first thing on his mind.

"The woman vamp."

"Ah." Alexi sat down on a log to Nathan's left. He had gotten dressed again after the vamp had left. Nathan must have really been distracted not to hear him coming back, and now he was blushing again at his mistake.

He was acting like a stupid teenager, and it kinda felt good. At least he wasn't so old that he wasn't capable of being pulled in by a fantastic female. She was the right package of outdoors and smoldering heat, and he was trying like hell to find out what the price tag might be. Not that he cared. If he did have what it cost, he would be spending it for the chance to know her better.

He just had a thousand pounds of uncle to deal with, a vamp who wasn't going to let him just move on with his life, and someone or many someones trying to take down his company. He needed to get his head screwed on straight, but his hormones were making that a stone-cold bitch to achieve. He had to grin at the reality that his world was going down the deep, dark hole of perdition, and he was going to smile all the way.

Alexi carried on with the conversation. "Yeah, she is a package. I wasn't sure what happened. She just appeared, took care of the first wolf without paying any attention to me, and went into the bushes to you guys like she was getting a little fresh air. Of course, all that blood on her face was a little frightening, even to me."

Alexi pulled the old coffeepot out of the ashes and retrieved a cup nearby. Pouring some dregs from the pot, he cupped the mug with both hands and took a small sip.

Nathan continued the story, "I was in bad straights. I was in a horrible tactical position, thinking I might try to join up with you against all three of them when in the middle of our fight she walks in, takes out the first wolf and demands we change. I'm a betting man, Alexi, but I never bet against vamps. I knew who she must be, but her coming here and daywalking surprised the hell out of me. I'm not ashamed to say I just laid down as quickly as gravity would take me and changed like a pup."

Alexi looked at Nathan. Taking in his size and stature, this man was a killer. That he was fighting two wolves, including that Alpha, and was mostly holding his own was a testament that he was no pushover. To have dropped his head and submissively shown his neck explained he knew power and respected it. That he had stood up for Ecaterina when questioning the vampire was something Alexi still considered.

It was obvious to Alexi that Nathan liked his niece. Hell, most everyone liked his niece, but she had wanderlust; she wasn't going to stay in the Brasov area. While he wouldn't want her to get caught up in this world, if she wasn't going to be wiped, she probably wouldn't find a better relationship for protection than this Were and the vamp. Well, if the vamp cared to protect her, that was. He needed to talk to Ecaterina and explain what was going on.

He got up. It was time to talk to her.

Nathan watched Alexi put his cup down and start toward Ecaterina. While he could sit right there and listen in to the conversation with his Were hearing, it would go badly when she realized what he had done later. He was sure she would buy a clue eventually, and then she would feel like he hadn't been respectful of her privacy. He stood up, went over to his rig, and got the last shirt.

Yelling to Alexi to let him know he was going to wash up a little, he left the clearing and headed for the lake.

That was where Bethany Anne found him.

Carpathian Mountains, Romania

Ecaterina wasn't doing much in her tent; mostly just hiding from the situation.

She had already changed her clothes, and the first aid Nathan had provided was sufficient. She had swallowed some pain relievers, and they were starting to take effect.

She was a little pissed that she had been taken so easily. With her eyes on where the shot had come from, she had not noticed the guy coming up behind her. She still wasn't sure how he had found her under the brush. She'd considered herself well hidden.

She supposed the mythology obviously had truth to it and they could sense more than she as a human could.

It wasn't as scary as she had thought it would be. She had thought people changing to wolves might be like that Michael Jackson video, painful and frightening. Since they just changed without grotesque bone reformation, stretching, and howling, that part was less off-putting than she would have guessed.

That her uncle was a bear was startling, but it explained his absence and why she had always felt safe in this area. She had seen his tracks from time to time, but they had never been too close, and while she had been careful, there had never been any feeling that the large bear was upset with her being up here.

Her hands were still shaking, and she had willed them to stop. She reminded them this wasn't how her family reacted, but that didn't cause them to still. Yeah, she was freaking out, but her body was handling the situation in her subconscious while her mind worked to piece everything together.

Then there was Nathan's obvious protectiveness as he had held her when the woman approached her, and his talking to her with the utmost respect. This was a woman Ecaterina wanted to know more about. This woman walked…well, she wasn't sure what way, but it was obvious that whatever path she took, it wasn't going to be a normal well-trodden one. It would be a path of excitement and stories she would not be part of if she stayed in Brasov.

She wanted to go with this woman—that was her decision. Her hands stilled, and she started pulling her gear together. Bethany Anne had said they were going to stay the night to make sure she was okay. Playing the weak woman card wouldn't score her any points, and frankly, it wasn't who Ecaterina was. Well, unless she was using it as bait.

She heard her uncle coming up behind her. She got out of the tent and started striking it.

She looked up at her uncle as she pulled a stake and saw the concern plainly written on his face. Dropping the stake, she walked to him while opening her arms. She could see he was trying not to scare her, and to give her space.

That wouldn't fly with her. This was her uncle, who had protected her and taken bullets for her—the guardian of the mountain. She wrapped him in her biggest, most loving hug, resting her head on his chest as he curled his arms around her. They stayed like that for a couple of minutes.

She stepped away and looked him in the eyes. "Thank you, Uncle. I care not what you are. I only care who you are in here." She touched his shirt over his heart.

"Ecaterina, my favorite niece." His eyes shone brightly with the relief that she gave him her love so willingly. "I'm sorry you were a part of this. If I had known anything was going to happen, I would have been up here last night. I am ashamed I didn't know about the pack." He looked around her space, noting that she had placed traps, some now dismantled, around where she had slept.

He sighed. "But I have to give you some information if you are going to survive the coming discussions. This woman...she is what we call a vampire. There are no good vampires, at least none that I know of. The best of them will leave you alone if you abide by their rules, but they don't suffer much, and the most powerful one will kill you as soon as look at you if you don't respect him. Please, can you hold that quick, spirited tongue of yours?" His eyes entreated her to answer the question "Yes."

"I do not have a spirited tongue! Mama just tells me that to make me more subservient so men will like me more." Her uncle raised an eyebrow as if she had just made his point.

Maybe she *was* a bit quick, she mused. Even Ivan occasionally suggested she not be so argumentative. "Okay, maybe I am a bit quick, but that is only with family."

Her uncle raised his other eyebrow.

She slumped. Who was she kidding? She loved a good verbal

fight. She hadn't felt scared around this woman, so she hadn't felt a need to be meek.

"Why is this so important, Uncle? What is she, who would have even you, as big as you can be, doing her bidding?" She crossed her arms, waiting for an answer.

Alexi looked around and realized Ecaterina had been packing. She obviously didn't want to stay here through the night. He was actually pleased to be going back to Brasov; he hadn't been home for a while. He started disabling the rest of the traps. You didn't want to leave them to hurt anything that might pass by if you wouldn't be checking them. A good hunter and trapper wouldn't do that.

Ecaterina finally joined him.

"These vampires—the strongest ones, the powerful ones—they are not like the stories. The weaker ones, yes, they are. But there are two groups, one good and one bad, yes?" He looked at her to make sure Ecaterina was listening. She was; Ecaterina knew how to strike camp in her sleep.

"None are fun to mess with. The good ones can be okay to deal with but are very touchy about their honor. The head of that family is named Michael. He is the one who created a list of rules when he found out about us; about the Wechselbalg. Most people, if they know anything about us, think of us as werewolves and werebears and other things. Pretty much we all talk that way, but that isn't what we *are*."

He finished disassembling the traps and placed the parts by the tree, so Ecaterina could find them again...if she ever made it back up to this mountain.

"I was told this happened centuries ago. Michael found the heads of the Wechselbalg and told them they had to find better ways to hide. There were too many stories of vampires and men who became wolves and preyed on people. His children were causing havoc at that time as well. He let it be known that if you let humans know what you were, you had to take care of the problem. If that meant the human had to die, then you killed them. He was busy for a while with two of his children who disappeared leaving too many young vampires—almost Nosferatu. He had to track down and dispatch dozens, and those two children were not seen again. It was difficult in those days to find anybody if they didn't want to be found. And I can tell you, those two did not want Michael to find them."

Ecaterina stopped filling her backpack. "Why is he considered the good side, if everyone is afraid of him and he killed so many that even his own children fled?"

"The stories say they felt they should be allowed to become the dominant species, rulers for all to swear fealty to. Michael didn't agree. Those children he has left and all *their* children have struggled to contain the Forsaken ever since. Now it is probably too late for the Forsaken to overtake any world power, with the weapons and technology they have. At least, I would think so."

"What about this one... This 'Bethany Anne?'"

Alexi's faraway look focused on Ecaterina. "Katia, you need to be careful with this one. She is powerful. I know from Nathan that she is a new vampire, and Michael chose her to become one of the family, but she is something different. She doesn't show the respect to Michael that every other vampire does. Something strange is going on here, and I don't know what. She isn't the same as any of the others I've heard stories about. She can walk in the sunlight, and only two can do that. She is dangerous, like all vampires, but even so, I don't know what to think about someone so new walking into a fight and ending it so quickly."

"Is she more powerful than the others? The other children?"

"I can't answer that. I don't know, and I have no idea what she wants yet. According to Nathan, he was sent here to find her and Michael. Now that he has found her, I think he just wants to lose her again."

"So he can go home? Back to America?" Ecaterina glanced at Nathan's tent.

Alexi, following her gaze, answered as casually as he could. "Maybe, maybe not. I think he has found a new thing he wants to learn more about. I don't believe he is going to be given much of a choice as to whether he can go back by himself—by the vampire, or this other interest he has." Alexi had to look toward the lake to keep Ecaterina from seeing his smile.

He heard a soft mumble, barely audible to even his enhanced hearing. "I wonder what he is so interested in?"

CHAPTER TWENTY-THREE

<u>Carpathian Mountains, Romania</u>

Bethany Anne was coming up on the clearing when she heard Nathan yell that he was going to the lake. She wanted to talk with him anyway, so she angled away and was waiting for the Were when he arrived at the shore.

She didn't hide from him; he knew she was there when he came out of the trees on the small path. He spoke easily to her, his voice a fine mellow sound.

"Hello again." Nathan took off his shirt, went to the cool, clear water, and used it as a rag to clean his upper body.

Bethany Anne noted he was ripped. His clothes did a good job hiding the muscles, but he had a chest to die for...well, if she *could*. Maybe Ecaterina would appreciate it? She knew there was a connection between them. It had been obvious as he treated her wounds, and Bethany Anne, who could appreciate a side of beefcake if it was going to wash right in front of her, didn't have the time or inclination to get involved romantically with everything else going on.

Although she could just about sneeze on the load of pheromones he was throwing off. He had it bad.

After washing a little, he turned toward Bethany Anne, who had just sat down. "I want to thank you for helping earlier. If you hadn't gotten involved, that group would have most likely taken Alexi and me out, and Ecaterina would probably have been hurt before she was killed. They wouldn't have wanted any witnesses, and Ecaterina isn't the type to just lie there and take it."

"You're welcome, but I wouldn't have killed Algerian if he hadn't disobeyed my order to stop and change. I wasn't protecting you; I was punishing disobedience. I suppose that worked out for you, in the end. I killed the sniper as the most expedient action, and I was a little unfocused. The first wolf was trying to get around Alexi and attack the girl. I wouldn't allow that to happen. The wolf I killed next to you had attacked me; it wasn't personal, and I needed the..." She didn't want to admit that she had needed the energy since she didn't know if anyone understood how her capabilities worked, so she finished her sentence, "Sustenance."

Her voice had a slight edge to it, which became harder the more she thought about the day's events.

"So, Mr. Lowell, were you sent here to search for Michael, and if so, by whom?"

Well, Nathan thought, *this is the tipping point*. He put on his other shirt and leaned against a rock about ten feet from Bethany Anne.

"I was asked as a favor to see if I could find you and Michael by a man by the name of Frank Kurns. He's the government representative who connects with the UnknownWorld groups. My company came under attack by what we thought were the Chinese, only to find out it was another group. Still not sure if it's vamps or Weres. He needed someone he could trust, and was able to solve a problem for me that put me in his immediate debt. I came over here to wipe the slate clean."

Bethany Anne stood up, wanting to think on her feet, and started pacing up and down the bank. Ten steps forward, ten steps back, repeat.

"What are you and Alexi, exactly?"

He was caught off-guard since he had assumed Bethany Anne knew about them. "Most call us 'Weres.'"

She stopped, looked him in the eyes, and raised an eyebrow. "Nathan, you don't go through any type of mutation from one form to the other that I could see. One second, you're one thing, the next you're something else. I have a general understanding of how to make a vampire, but I'm completely clueless when it comes to, well…to you Weres." She resumed her pacing.

Nathan watched her for a minute, then scratched his chin. "Well, we have another name, which is 'Wechselbalg.' It's German, and means 'changeling.' Don't know if that helps or not. We have the whole conservation of mass issue with the different sizes. I'm not much for waving a wand over the whole thing and saying 'magic,' but I've done as much research as possible and haven't figured anything out. You say you know how vampires are made?"

He was just trying to keep the conversation going. He was certainly not trying to get the inside information on vamps and how to make—and potentially unmake—them.

Bethany Anne didn't rise to the bait. "Yes. Yes, I do, and no, I won't be sharing that with you right now. Not knowing how you change will be an itch I need to scratch until I understand it. Not to get personal with you, but how old are you?" She stopped pacing and looked at him again, her eyes suddenly very serious and watchful.

God, he thought, *I hate vampires*. "I'm a little over eighty-four." Next she was going to be asking him about robbing the cradle.

She raised an eyebrow. "You're a very energetic eighty-four, Mr. Lowell."

Nathan couldn't understand why she switched back and forth from his first name to his last name. It was off-putting—and maybe that was the whole reason: to keep him on his toes. Well, since she wasn't trying to drain him of blood, it was going to take a lot more than just changing which name she was using to fluster him.

"Yeah, Wechselbalg are pretty long-lived. Depending on how much time we stay as our animal, we can live between the longest span of a normal human to two hundred and forty years, and occasionally more."

It was his turn, he decided. "Since you seemed to be a little upset with Michael, I surmise you haven't seen him lately—or have you seen too much of him?"

She again resumed pacing. "Yeah, are you talking about my comment about cleaning up his bullshit?"

Nathan didn't correct her; that was close enough.

"No, I don't know where he is, so from that standpoint, Frank might know more about it than me. He left six or seven months ago, and I haven't seen him since. Why does Frank want you to find him so badly?"

"Well, Frank was tracking Michael's personal plane. Carl was using it. You know Carl?" She nodded that she did. "The plane disappeared over the English Channel, no bodies or wreckage found. Frank worked with Carl to get things cleaned up; certain things that Michael's Family is better equipped to handle, and it isn't happening without a contact. Carl was the contact, and the family isn't moving without the threat of Michael hanging over their heads. Frank has lost a fair number of people trying to keep a lid on the...problems."

"Are we talking monsters, Mr. Lowell? Are these the problems that Michael's Family took care of, the ones even the black-ops combat groups are cautious with?"

"Yes, probably."

"Okay, and you, Mr. Lowell? Tell me about Nathan Lowell. Why are you someone Frank Kurns feels comfortable talking with? No need to be humble; I'd like the real dirt."

Oh, fuckity fuck. Life had just taken a left turn into gibbering concern. He didn't want to tell this lady anything more about himself. He wanted to go home. Okay, maybe after a few more days with Ecaterina he would want to go home. Probably. Perhaps...

Maybe the two of them could sneak out together? Nathan snorted. Like he had Alexi fooled.

Nathan went ahead and told her everything that was even vaguely relevant to the situation. He glossed over his different companies and explained that his main company did security for digital communications, hoping she didn't clue in too much to what that actually was. He wasn't going to bet he'd pulled one over on her, but he could claim he mentioned it.

"So, you are the second to the main Alpha of all packs in the US, correct? Good. I can work with that."

Damn, translate that to, "I can work with you," or better: "You will work for me, slave!" Nathan sighed.

"Don't look so down, Mr. Lowell. Carl told me about Frank, so I know he can be trusted. I'm piggybacking Frank's reputation onto you. I need a contact to help me get into the game, and you're it. Frank's payback is going to take longer."

Nathan felt like he had just won the nomination to be the first runner sent on a suicide mission. "How long might this go on? I do have those aforementioned businesses to run."

"Until we find Carl alive, or I can replace you. Your concerns about your business are duly noted, and we will look into that situation. I need your focus to be on helping me sort this fuster-cluck out."

"You do know the vampires aren't going to want to talk to me, right? Vampires don't have a high opinion of Weres. Well, anyone really, so I guess I can't make that a hate crime particular to Weres."

"Nathan, by the time I finish with the local vampire Family, they will be the politest group you have ever met."

Nathan couldn't stop the snort before it escaped his nose. Ah damn, he had been doing so well.

"Not finding that very likely, Mr. Lowell?"

Crap, thought Nathan, back to his last name again. "Let's just say my eight decades have provided a one-sided... No, make that a *very singular* experience when it comes to how vampires treat other species."

"Yeah, I got that impression already. How did Michael keep everyone in line?"

"Lots of pain and death."

It was her turn to snort. "Well, I could do without the death part. But if you crack a few rotten eggs, maybe the rest of the carton will get the message. In fact, I'm counting on that happening. I think we'll start with Petre, then check on Stephen."

"Are you going alone?"

"Why? Are you offering your services, Mr. Lowell?"

"I might be able to help with Petre's children, but he's probably too much for me to handle."

"Well, I'm not sure how much I will need your physical prowess, Nathan. But I will certainly need your cybersecurity skills. Have you ever been on the darknet, Nathan?"

Well crap, he thought, she hadn't been fooled one bit.

"Yes, I'm familiar with it all. I was on the front line of hacking and cracking with early modems, and enjoyed it. That was how I started my consulting business. I might have a few old personas lying around."

Bethany Anne grinned suddenly. It was a nice grin...until it turned feral. "Wonderful. In fact, I'd love to talk with ID10T-42. Would you happen to know him?"

Nathan, who had made the mistake of getting comfortable talking with a vampire, realized it had been a setup the whole time. How she knew one of his hacking personas was beyond him. She might be able to read his mind, for all he knew. He wasn't sure exactly what a vampire could do, especially this one. "Yeah. Yeah, I guess I can get you in contact with him."

"Good to know. I'll need *him* to get me all the security information possible on Petre and his home and offices to figure out how and where to introduce myself. I'm not sure if I'll go for sneaky or upfront yet."

"You know the family doesn't appreciate anyone killing their own, right?"

"Nathan, thank you for the warning, but the previous methods of instruction haven't seemed to work. I'm going to implement a new instruction regimen, and I fully expect to have a few conversations before its acceptance. If I go to Stephen first, it will seem like I need his approval. When I reprimand Petre, it will send the right message."

Nathan thought, Oh, it'll send a message all right. He hoped she wanted to send the message, "This lady is suicidal."

Nathan and Bethany Anne walked back to the clearing, making enough noise that Alexi and Ecaterina could hear them approach.

Bethany Anne was good with going back early. Her only concern was Ecaterina's health, and the girl seemed to be just fine. With a proper guide and the ability of three of them to easily see in the darkness, they made good time.

Nathan had used his phone when he had a good connection to call Ivan and let Ecaterina explain what they needed. Ivan came to the pickup point in a white van without any passenger windows. Ivan and Alexi rode up front, leaving Ecaterina, Nathan, and Bethany Anne hidden in the back in case anyone was still looking for them.

Nathan called Frank and left a coded message that he was "getting close." Bethany Anne didn't want to make direct contact with Frank until after she had taken care of the Petre situation. One complication at a time.

Nathan assumed his stuff back at the hotel was a write-off. Given that the pack members had not come back from the mountain, he was sure it would be watched. Bethany Anne considered going after it herself, but it would let the pack—and therefore Petre—know she was in town.

Ivan was able to get them into a basement that had a good internet connection. There were two couches, not so comfortable, and one bedroom and full bathroom for the four of them.

After about a day in the confined space—and with the tension increasing exponentially—Bethany Anne felt like slapping both guys. When she realized they were both worried about her going all vampy on Ecaterina's neck, she had her first bout of uncontrolled laughter since waking up in the medical Pod. The men just looked at each other at first, perplexed, until Bethany Anne was able to explain she didn't need daily blood to survive. Her ripping heads off and sucking blood from necks was related to the fight and the massive expenditure of energy.

Resting in the room was a net gain for her, so there was no need for them to stress about protecting Ecaterina.

Ecaterina thought it a little childish of the men to get all protective of her. She had been taking care of herself in the mountains for almost all of her twenty-four years, and suddenly she had these two guys suffocating her.

Ecaterina asked Bethany Anne about what she had done before she came to Europe, so Bethany Anne shared her work in the CIA and, without naming names, her work in her former agency.

Nathan's hacker persona came through with a location the second morning, finding some plans for a nice little two story with basement a little outside the city, which was situated on its own land. There were some notes about extra security being in place, but the only thing Nathan could confirm were some bills paid to a local security-systems installation company fourteen months previously.

They talked it over, and it was decided that Alexi and Ecaterina would go and take a look at the house. They had the best woodscraft. Nathan might be excellent in the woods, but he didn't know how to look for traps. The Brasov pack would know if another wolf they scented was part of their pack. Alexi was a known local, and while they might be concerned, at least he lived in the area.

Ecaterina going out like this didn't sit too well with Nathan, but he was a big enough boy to know when to keep his mouth shut.

To keep Nathan busy, Bethany Anne had him researching Stephen's territory and attempting to find any banking-related information for Petre. Trainers always said, "Trace the money to find out what's important in a man's life."

Well, it worked when she was tracking dirt on politicians, anyway.

Brasov, Romania

They compared notes when Alexi and Ecaterina returned later that evening. They didn't want to chance Petre getting involved, and their best guess was he would be up at night. Sitting on the two couches, they went over the results from their reconnaissance of Petre's house.

They had found a few regular traps and then hit the electronic versions. Petre was well-protected from anything coming through the woods.

"Damn." Bethany Anne seemed a little annoyed that Petre would make this hard for her. "I don't know enough about this guy to decide if I can just walk up and slap him around, or if he has enough muscle on the property to make life difficult."

Nathan piped up, "Have you considered the Brasov pack?"

"No, not really. They're in the back of my mind, but unless they all jump me at the same time, I should be able to fight my way clear of them." Bethany Anne was quiet for a minute.

Nathan considered her comment. If she could take on that many at one time, just how strong was she already? If a child of

Michael's had become this powerful in less than a year, how strong was Stephen?

"What if, beyond your ability to make Stephen see reason, he decides you have to pay for Petre? I still don't like that you aren't just taking the problem up with him." Nathan wasn't happy that they were going outside the normal channels. He didn't know what Michael would do to Bethany Anne for going around the established protocols and felt obligated to continue to encourage her to consider changing her plan.

Bethany Anne considered his comment...for at least the fourth time. She respected that he came from a culture where this was literally a life or death decision, and his trepidation was rooted in that culture.

"I'm not going to effect change by following the old rules. Because of Michael's influence vampires only understand power, at the end of the day—Michael's power. Michael and I talked about this on the trip over here. It was very rare that an attack would happen on American soil because Michael would get involved if Bill couldn't take care of the issue. So, whoever out there is making this happen, they're confident in their ability to take on Michael and his family.

"I've thought about this for a while. I think the Forsaken have become empowered by a new way to attack. From the footage and what Michael knows about a situation in World War II, there's apparently a method to create a form of zombie Nosferatu. They're intelligent enough to handle fairly complicated instructions, but they don't have a will of their own. The ones in the explosion which killed Bill didn't hesitate to blow themselves up."

Nathan considered what Bethany Anne had just shared. "If they're Nosferatu, that pretty much makes them Forsaken, right? None of Michael's children allow a changed person to live if they don't make it past that stage."

"Unless we have another child or set of children who have decided to break from Michael, yes. I asked Michael why they hadn't just bombed his residence in America, and he said that, while possible, it would have been difficult for them to do anything permanent to him. There are so many video cameras in town that they would have a good chance of finding who had done it. Plus, vampires never sleep where they don't have a bolt-hole."

Ecaterina spoke up for the first time since they explained what they had found at Petre's house. "What is 'bolt-hole?' I don't understand this word."

Nathan jumped in. "It means 'a way out.' A second—or third—way for him to leave the house, usually underground, which comes out far away."

"So if we find this bolt-hole, he will come out there if his house is attacked?"

Bethany Anne took this question. "Yes. If I went through his house and he got concerned before I got to him, he could slip away. Then I would have a bigger problem on my hands."

"So, this bolt-hole is probably outside protected area. Uncle and I go and try to find exit and close it, if possible."

Bethany Anne thought about that, and she noticed that Nathan was grimacing. He didn't like the idea much.

"Okay, here's what we can do: I need you and your uncle to go back and see if you can find any exits. They'll be very hard to spot. If you can find one, we will probably do this. If you can find two, then I feel it's better than fifty-fifty that we can contain Petre. I can get into the house during the day when he's probably sleeping. If he tries to flee, he'll have the sun to deal with, so he would prefer to either get out in a closed van or something similar, or hide in the house until the sun goes down.

"I'll need a reason to be there. I don't think they'll allow me to just walk up, and if I do something vampy I will lose the element of surprise."

Just then Nathan leaned toward her and sniffed. She raised an eyebrow at him.

"You don't smell like a vampire. I just realized that. I knew you were a vampire when you first came into the bushes, but you don't have that..." Her glare dared him to continue that sentence. "You don't smell like a vampire, is all I'm trying to say."

She was about to give Nathan a small tongue-lashing when she realized Alexi was leaning toward her surreptitiously from beside Ecaterina. "What the hell is wrong with you two?"

Alexi answered her as he leaned back. "It's how we know someone is a vampire if they aren't being...what did you call it? Yes, 'vampy.' All vampires smell like old blood, yes?"

Bethany Anne scrunched her nose. "I heard about that, but I haven't smelled a vampire since getting the olfactory upgrade, so I don't personally know. I hope you two have had enough smelling; you're making me want to take another bath." She got up and started pacing between the two couches, dictating how she wanted the effort to go. They broke the meeting up, and the two trackers took baths and went to bed. They would be getting up early to be in a position to look around when dawn broke. They each carried a cell phone, so they could text when they found anything.

That next morning, right after Ecaterina and Alexi had left to meet Ivan at one of his many equipment stashes, Nathan and Bethany Anne discussed how he would approach the house with Bethany Anne as a "prisoner." They had decided to blame Alexi for the pack deaths. The story was that Nathan wanted to trade his life for Bethany Anne. Since she was the new chosen child, she should be worth it, right? Since she smelled human, that should get them in the door.

At first, Nathan got a little righteous about his honor. He would never trade a woman for his life. Bethany Anne smiled a little at the realization that she was becoming a person to Nathan, not just something to be feared.

She also got out of him that he didn't like the fact that if word went around he didn't play straight-up, it wouldn't go well for him in future negotiations. She pointed out that he was a hacker, among other things, and she didn't believe he had a lily-white reputation now.

He rebutted that he wasn't his hacker personas, and that no one knew those 'highly intelligent workers for freedom of information' were him.

She shut him up by observing that the dead wouldn't talk—or be concerned about what people said about them.

After the obligatory grumbling from Nathan, they got ready and then got into their vehicle. They would drive to within about three miles of his house and walk the rest of the way since they didn't want to have their vehicle tracked. Petre's house was on a small private road, anyway.

They were in the car a little before 9:00 AM when they got the first text that Ecaterina had found an entrance. She and Alexi were still looking.

Bethany Anne didn't like how easy it had been to find the first exit. Nathan championed Ecaterina's abilities; it had been why he'd paid so much for her skills.

Bethany Anne had already gotten the story from Ivan, so she knew how Nathan had been suckered into paying for the trip in advance. While she let his comment go without correcting him, she thought it was cute that he was trying to pump up Ecaterina's skill. She was pretty sure Nathan would be shooting for Ecaterina to be on the team when they left Brasov.

A little after noon, she got a text that they had found a separate and much better-hidden exit. Alexi had changed to his bear form and smelled around until he had caught a musty scent and, of all things, the odor of French fries coming out of a large clump of bushes. It was agreed that Alexi would remain in bear form and push against the metal door at the bottom of some poorly-poured concrete stairs behind the bushes. Petre was almost certainly strong, but it was incredibly unlikely he would be able to move Alexi.

Alexi had sent Ecaterina to watch the other exit.

It was time.

Nathan and Bethany Anne got out of the car. Nathan took a couple of plastic ties, and after walking a little way down the path, he found what he was looking for. He looked at Bethany Anne. "You sure you can handle your anger? I don't want to suddenly get dead doing what you told me to do."

Bethany Anne smiled at the comment. "Yeah, I'm good. I won't feel a thing. Are you okay throwing down a defenseless woman?"

Nathan grabbed Bethany Anne's arms and held them behind her back as he zipped the ties in place. "I am absolutely NOT okay with hurting a defenseless woman. In fact, it goes against my masculinity."

Grinning behind her back, Nathan used his substantial strength and pushed Bethany Anne so hard she flew into some thorny bushes, rolling ass over appetite and getting her clothes, face, and hands torn up until she fetched up against a tree. From about twenty-five feet away from the road, Nathan heard, "You sonofabitch! I'm defenseless here!"

Nathan smiled widely. "But Bethany Anne, you're not a woman!"

A few minutes later—after Nathan decided it was safe enough to get close to Bethany Anne again— he was pleased with how messed up she looked. Plant debris covered her clothes, a small branch and leaves were still in her hair, and she had dirt and scratches over her eyes and cheeks.

The death glare she gave him was just the right touch. He decided she looked just like a human who was pissed, but not in a position to do anything about it.

His life was complete, or as complete as it would get until they made it through this operation. It was a shame he wouldn't ever be able to share the story of shoving a vampire into a tree without living to regret it.

Bethany Anne barely opened her lips, her voice soft. "If this look doesn't get us in, I'm taking you out back and beating you against a few trees to get my anger out. You feel me, Mr. Lowell?"

Nathan's glimmer of good humor wasn't diminished by her threat. "I believe I *will* feel it, Ms. Reynolds. I trust that I will. But if this plan doesn't work, I'm not sure I'll be alive to worry about it."

"Oh, I'll make sure you stay alive just so I can get my pound of your flesh. That shove was fucking hard. My teeth almost went out the back of my head, you prick." All Bethany Anne got for her verbal tirade was a wider smile out of Nathan.

They walked up to the entrance. The twelve-foot-high metal gates opened in the middle and were bracketed by large concrete columns with the letter 'P' in Cyrillic on each, topped with gas lanterns that were lit. The walls extended about fifteen feet in each direction before just stopping. If she wanted to, she could just walk around the walls. It looked so stupid.

Except that there were probably traps over there.

Nathan hit the call button on the security post.

Nothing.

He hit it again, and a guy came on and spoke in Russian.

Nathan replied in English, "I don't understand that Russian shit. Anyone speak English in there?"

"Yeah, yeah, I speak English too. What do you want?"

"I'm Nathan Lowell, and I ran into some people up on the mountain. I want to make a trade."

"One moment."

One moment had become two minutes before another, more cultured voice, came on. "Who is this?"

Bethany Anne kept the pissed-off countenance going. It wasn't hard to fake; she was getting impatient. She assumed they had video, so the acting needed to be as real as possible...and Nathan had already supplied her with a superior reason to be pissed off.

"Nathan Lowell."

"And you would want what exactly, Mr. Lowell?" Nathan decided he was speaking with Petre.

"I need to speak with Petre. I have something he wants, and in exchange, I want a free pass back to the States."

"And where are my partners, Mr. Lowell?"

"Are you Petre?" Nathan got silence for his answer. Yup, he was talking with a vampire. Weres would get angry, but most of them would have said something. "They aren't among the living, I'm afraid. They had a fight with a werebear on the mountain. He was protecting two women. I have one with me, and the other one was killed with the other pack members."

"And what do you have for me, Mr. Lowell?"

"I have the child Michael was going to use to create the replacement for Bill, who was destroyed in the United States."

"What do I want with her, Mr. Lowell?"

"Well, I wouldn't rightly know, Petre. That's vampire Family business, not something I need to be privy to." Nathan wanted to vomit in his mouth. He wasn't stupid around vampires, but he knew enough about this prick that it galled him to have to act as if he respected him in any way.

"I see. I'm going to open the gate. Please be sure you stay on the path; I don't want to have to smell your remains after they get blown all over my beautiful trees." The speaker squelched.

Nathan grabbed Bethany Anne's arm and pulled her toward the opening gate. "C'mon, you whiny bitch, let's get my ticket out of this country."

"Whiny bitch?" Bethany Anne kicked him *hard*, and he started limping and cursing fluently and loudly. He turned like he was going to backhand her, then took one look at her eyes and remembered to act disgusted as he grabbed her arm again.

The house was large, with a three-car garage on the lower right and very little glass showing. Made of poured concrete, it looked pretty modern to his eyes.

The front door opened as they walked up to it, and two men

came out. Both had underarm holsters, but neither had his hand on his gun.

The air blowing out the house had a putrid scent Bethany Anne hadn't smelled before.

That would be a vampire odor.

That's making me want to gag. Is that it? What a stench. Can't humans smell that?

Your auditory sense is very acute, and the air in there is saturated from Petre living there. His scent gets stronger the longer he lives.

They stopped in front of the two men. One was in a pair of jeans and a sports jacket, and the other had on an old Members Only jacket. Bethany Anne could barely bite her tongue in time to keep from making a scathing fashion-choice comment.

The one with the Members Only jacket took Bethany Anne's arm and glanced at her disheveled appearance, scuffed face and the debris tangled hair and then back at Nathan.

"What?" the Were exclaimed defensively. "She's a whiny bitch. Sue me." Bethany Anne's eyes got a little narrower.

That same cultured voice met them at the door. "Mr. Lowell, you should take care how you speak about anyone in the family."

Nathan looked at Petre. He was a normal-sized guy about four inches shorter than the Were and had a lean swimming-pool body with wider shoulders and a slender waist, compared to Nathan's bulked-up physique. His black hair was cut really short, and he wore a designer athletic suit. He looked a little rumpled for a vampire. They had probably woken him up.

"I figured she wasn't a Family member yet, so my apologies."

"Oh, she isn't. If she was, I would have had to kill you. You realize we won't tolerate disrespect to the Family, right?" There was a dangerous glint of amusement in Petre's eyes, like he found the words loathsome to say out loud without a sardonic smile at the same time to give the lie to his statement.

"My apologies. Again, can I go now?"

"No, not yet, Mr. Lowell. Please come in and enjoy my hospitality while you tell me the whole story about what happened to my associates. We will need to go back and find them for a proper funeral, of course."

Nathan didn't let anything show on his face, but this wasn't something they had considered. He hoped Bethany Anne would go berserk on them so they could get this over with. He wanted a real bed to collapse on for a couple of days, preferably with a certain someone for company—if he could find a way to get rid of her uncle. Maybe if he put down steaks Alexi would gorge on, then go hibernate for a week.

They walked into the house past an office and the kitchen. There was another room that seemed to be ready for painting since a tarp covered the floor. Petre had stopped in the kitchen while the guy with Bethany Anne took her to the room with the tarp.

"I will need your information, Mr. Lowell. I doubt Ms. Reynolds will be able to provide me with much in the way of answers." Petre reached over the bar as Nathan was walking past him.

Suddenly he heard a room-thundering *boom* and Bethany Anne, a hole through her torso and blood splattering the wall behind her, fell to the floor.

Nathan jumped to the side and looked at Petre, who had a twinkle in his eye as he lowered his weapon. He looked at Nathan with an eyebrow raised. "Vampire politics. You understand, right, Nathan?"

Gott Verdammt vampires, especially the psychotic ones!

Both pack guys turned to Nathan with dark gleams in their eyes. Their animals were apparently close to coming out.

"Now, Mr. Lowell, why don't we discuss where my associates can find their packmates?"

Something moved in the other room and both pack members stared, as did Petre, when Bethany Anne stood up. The gaping red hole in her torso was big enough to see the blood-spattered wall through it. Her eyes had turned red again, like they had been when Nathan had first encountered her on the mountain.

There didn't seem to be any intelligence behind those eyes. Nathan started thinking about how the hell he could get out of there without being noticed by Bethany Anne when Petre lifted the gun again. Without thinking, he leaped to smack Petre's arm aside. The gun fired once into the bar and the vampire back-handed Nathan into a wall five feet away.

Nathan hit the wall and landed on his knees, coughing and working to get his breath back. There was anger in his eyes, and he couldn't stop his mouth. "Petre, you hit like a girl."

But there was no Petre to hear him. Nathan looked at Bethany Anne. She had been attacked by both of the pack goons, and she'd ripped off Members Only Guy's left arm. He was screaming in pain on the floor. The better-dressed one was struggling with the significantly smaller woman's arms as she casually chewed on his neck, blood spraying both of them. The hole in her torso was healing at a rapid rate. She dropped the listless guy on the floor and knelt by the other thug, who was slowing down and looked to be going into shock. His healing ability was trying to stop the bleeding from his stump. Bethany Anne snapped her fingers in front of his eyes to get his attention

Frightened, he looked up at her as she wiped a finger across his bleeding arm socket and licked it off.

"Where is the bolt-hole?" All she got was a guy shaking his head spasmodically.

"Where is he going?" Her voice was silk over steel, and her gaze pierced his soul.

"Downstairs. He lives downstairs. Left through the kitchen, then behind the mirror at the end of the hall."

"Good. I hope you yell when you get there."

The guy looked confused. "Where? Where am I going?"

Bethany Anne slapped his head, causing blood to explode all

over the wall. The rest of the head, with his unseeing eyes, rebounded off the wall and landed on the other side of the room. "To hell."

She stood up, looked around, told Nathan to check out the rest of the house. Then she calmly walked around him and headed after Petre.

CHAPTER TWENTY-FOUR

Brasov, Romania

Ecaterina heard her uncle's roaring and realized Petre was trying to get out through his exit. They were prepared if he tried to come out during the day, but she was hoping he stayed over by her uncle. She was determined to pull her weight. She hadn't appreciated anything this Petre had done to her and her family, not to mention her new friends.

When the noise continued, she took it to be a good sign. If Uncle Alexi was battling the vampire, Petre wouldn't come her way.

That was what she was thinking when the noise stopped.

She wasn't strong enough or quick enough to fight a vampire, so hopefully, all her years in the wild had prepared her for this situation. She decided to set the final bait.

They had found the exit she was watching easily enough. It wasn't hidden too well, just a small pile of detritus for conceal-ment. This was a throwaway exit, only there to hopefully capture the attention of a backup group, keeping their focus away from the better-hidden second exit. She would have never been able to find the main exit on her own. It was concealed too well.

The wooden door started to creak, and there were successive jerky pushes to get the old leaves and dirt off it as it opened.

Petre, hiding under a very heavy dark cloak, came out of the hole and turned around to see if anyone was there. He quickly spotted Ecaterina and was struck dumb. He moved toward her.

Seconds later, Bethany Anne heard Petre's high scream of pain. She had found the entrance to the underground tunnels and was moving quickly through them, keeping her left hand against the wall. She was barely able to judge distance in the dank, dark tunnel. When she heard the screaming, she took the tunnel that led her in that direction.

At her enhanced speed and with better light (she hadn't thought to bring a flashlight), she finished the last hundred or so yards in a few seconds. The end of the tunnel was considerably brighter since the door at the end wasn't properly shut.

It didn't hurt that she could hear Petre's cussing and then a loud, meaty whack and a body hitting the ground.

Not knowing what she would find, she practically threw the trap door off in a shower of splinters, only to find Petre slumped on the ground with his foot in a bear trap and Ecaterina slowly buttoning her shirt. It was obvious she had no bra on—and it didn't look like one was necessary.

Gazing at Bethany Anne, Ecaterina finished the last button on her shirt and bent over to pick up a large metal cross. "What? Father always say to use the right bait. He not even look down."

Bethany Anne burst out laughing as Alexi came running through the trees calling Ecaterina's name.

Shaking her head, Bethany Anne easily pried open the bear trap. Petre was a mess inside his robe and clothes, and there was blood all over his broken left leg. She found a holstered .45 while patting him down and took it out, considered whether he had enough damage, and casually shot him in the other leg. She slid the gun into her waistband after setting the safety.

Petre didn't make a sound as she threw him back into the

tunnel, just landed with a thud. If she was lucky, she had just broken his damn neck. She told Alexi to hold the fort for a few minutes; they would call if everything was good with Nathan.

She jumped down into the tunnel and spotted an old light switch, which she clicked on. Very dim red lights came on about every fifty feet, enough for a vampire to see easily. Grabbing Petre's foot, she started walking down the tunnel toward the house. She stayed alert in case he should wake up, but she didn't care if he hit more rocks on the way back to the house. In fact, she steered with purpose and knocked Petre's head against two large rocks on the side of the tunnel.

She had read somewhere about how to live a purpose-driven life. She figured she'd just had a purpose-driven moment and could work up from there.

Brasov, Romania

When she got back to the house with Petre, his bullet wound was healed enough to stop bleeding, and it looked like his leg was getting better. The swelling on his head wound was going down too.

She exited the tunnels into an office, where the door was hidden behind a bookcase. She gave him ten demerits for lack of evil-lair-exit originality. He had a cricket bat signed by the Romanian cricket team on a wall display, so she grabbed it, and went back to Petre, who was starting to stir. She calmly palmed the bat in her right hand and slammed it down on Petre's forehead. He stopped moving.

His souvenir bat now had a little dent where it had connected with his head, and some of the signatures were smeared. She decided she liked this bat. She grabbed Petre's left leg with her unencumbered hand, dragged him back through the house, and dropped him in the room with the tarp where he had shot her.

Poetic justice, she thought.

When she returned with Petre, Nathan was coming downstairs with two laptops in his hands. She raised her eyebrows.

Nathan quickly asked his most pressing concern. "And Ecaterina... Or Alexi... Are they okay?"

"Yes. You should be proud of our Ecaterina. She trapped Petre when he came out of the exit she was responsible for after he couldn't get past Alexi's door. He literally never looked at the bear trap that caught his foot."

Nathan stood there, a puzzled expression on his face. "Bear trap? Wouldn't he have been paying attention? Those aren't easy to hide."

"Not when he was staring at Ecaterina's bare tits. I'm sure he never noticed anything above her neck or below her navel. I heard the screams, and by the time I found the end of the tunnel she had hit him with an old rusted iron cross. When I got out, she was already buttoning up her shirt and picking up the cross again. You should have been there."

Nathan's face was classic guy—slack-jawed with a thousand-yard stare—so she snapped her fingers in front of his face. "What did you find out? what's with the laptops?"

Shaking it off, Nathan answered, "Found them in a safe in his bedroom. Idiot never changed the safe's original combination from the manufacturer. I'm going to put them into a clean room and see what we can get off them."

"Anything else?"

"No, nothing. These two dead guys can't tell us anything."

"We'll get it out of Petre as soon as I let him wake up."

"*Let* him?"

"I found a cricket bat. I'm still pissed at getting shot. That shit fucking *hurt*."

"Yeah, I was able to see right through you. Why didn't that take you out?" Nathan was pretty sure he didn't know of any vampire stories where that kind of damage wouldn't have hurt the vampire, especially such a young vampire, significantly more. She certainly shouldn't have been able to stand up.

"Tale for another time."

"When?"

"About thirty minutes after I trust you more. Now stop being nosy and help me figure out a way to stage this house so they don't come looking for DNA evidence."

Seemed like she had the normal vampire trust issues. Or, Nathan conceded, she could have been this way before the V-change.

He looked at all the blood. Even if they took up the tarp, they couldn't clean this house enough that a CSI group wasn't going to get her blood. "Not going to happen. There's no way they can see the arterial spray and not realize something else went on. Shit, there's a damn hole in the wall with half your stomach in it."

She looked where he was pointing. That was just gross—her insides sprayed across the wall.

TOM, are the authorities going to find the nanocytes in my blood that's all over this room?

No. Within an hour your blood won't be recognizable, and the organs that are presently on display are decomposing at a very fast rate. So long as no one throws them into a cryogenic vat, nothing here will be traceable to you, and no nanocytes will remain.

More than likely the pack would find this place before the cops. By the time she was done with Petre, there wouldn't be any DNA evidence left for them, if they were even called. If it was true about the sun turning them into ash, she'd get a broom to make sure Petre wasn't a recognizable lump. Otherwise, she'd toss him into the house.

But Nathan's scent was all over this house. Looked like it would be fire, then. Even if the house didn't burn completely, the smoke would be enough to mask Nathan's scent.

"Nathan, did you find any money in the safe?"

"Yeah, enough to get us all first-class tickets back to the States, and a little extra. I also found a few pieces of jewelry, not sure whose. Some paperwork and insurance documents, and house documents and the like. Nothing but the laptops, money, and jewelry seemed important."

"Okay. We can use the money to get out of Romania without using credit cards, and if we need bribes to get across the border."

Nathan looked at her and smiled. "I think you're still remembering being human. I don't think you need to worry about getting across the border. You could just run past them, and they wouldn't see you."

"Until they looked at the video, sure. But I get your point. What about you?"

"Me? I can just change and run across and meet up with you on the other side."

"What about Ecaterina?"

"She's going?" Nathan's interest was piqued.

"If she wants to. She held her own and stopped a vampire. That's pretty gutsy in my book. Granted, he wasn't the shiniest tool in the shed, but she didn't know that. I wish I could have seen Petre's eyes when that bear trap crunched his leg."

"Speaking of Petre, what do you want to do with him?"

"I'm going to talk with him, but I'll do that alone. You can help me by finding fuel you can use to start a fire. Your smell is all over this house, so I want all the rooms to go up in flames when I'm done."

"What about your…" He waved a hand toward the wall.

"Won't be a problem by the time we leave. Call Ecaterina and Alexi, and let them know we'll meet them back at the room to grab our stuff and decide where to go next. I don't want them here in the house. Did you find any video?"

"No. They actually didn't *have* any video."

"Hmmm…"

Nathan was reminded of the "whiny bitch" comment and decided a tactical retreat was in order. "I'm just going to go and find that fuel."

Bethany Anne watched him leave. "You just do that." She went over to Petre and thought about whacking him one more time for good measure, but decided she needed to get answers and get back to Brasov.

Now, what would be the best way to motivate a sun-fearing vampire? She grabbed one of Petre's legs and started toward the front door. "You know, Petre, you should have put on a little more sunscreen this morning. I'm thinking you're about to get a serious sunburn. Watch the doorstep. Damn, that had to hurt—if you were awake to feel it, anyway."

Nathan came back into the kitchen in time to hear Bethany Anne muttering at the comatose Petre as she pulled his body through the front door, down the step, and around the corner.

"Michael was either a genius or suffering from a mental lapse when he chose that woman," he mused aloud.

Bethany Anne yelled, "I heard that!"

Nathan got busy splashing the gasoline he'd found in the garage around the kitchen. "Well, fuckity fuck. The walk back is going to suck."

Her voice was soft, and right behind his ear. "Don't make me pull off one of Petre's legs and beat your disrespectful ass, Mr. Lowell." Nathan turned around, but she was already gone.

Nathan kept his mouth shut after that.

Brasov, Romania

Alexi, Ecaterina, and Ivan were in the basement when Nathan and Bethany Anne got back. Nathan immediately went to take a shower, since the smoke was bothering his nose.

Alexi had been explaining his life to both his niece and

nephew; how he had been mauled as a child and healed up in a winter season when he shouldn't have completely healed. He hadn't told the others in their family, for good reason. Regardless of how Bethany Anne felt, he required them to give their word that they would not pass it on to others in the family. Ivan was good leaving this whole experience behind him if he could, but he could tell his sister wanted to know more. Her closeness to the natural realm just inflamed her excitement about people who could get even closer to nature than she could. She had a driving need to know more and be more.

There was someone who could tell her more, but he had just gone to take a shower. There was one other person who could and would stop what she intended to do with merely a word, so when Bethany Anne came in she excused herself and walked over to her.

She asked Bethany Anne for a moment of her time, feeling trepidation. Her future could be changed just by asking for the chance to do more. What would Bethany Anne say? Was her help with capturing Petre enough? Would she do what Nathan had talked about and follow this Michael's rules and make her forget? She was throwing the dice. If she stayed here in Brasov, she could learn more from her uncle, maybe find a way to safely change herself and feel the wind through her hair as she walked through the forests as a bear.

She had considered that idea seriously, but right now there was another she wanted to be with and learn more about. He was a man after her own heart...and so much more.

She feared he might eventually give in to Bethany Anne. The vampire was exquisite—beyond beautiful—and she knew that if it wasn't for the scary-vampire part, Nathan would be attracted to her. Besides, if Ecaterina wasn't close enough for Nathan to focus on, he would do what all men did and start losing his brain cells. His brain would stop reminding him how dangerous and deadly

Bethany Anne was; all he would remember was the perfect female package she presented—at least when she wasn't beating people with their own arms that she had pulled off a moment before.

They went upstairs and sat at the table in the kitchen. Ecaterina started, "I want to thank you for all you have done helping my uncle and me with these packs and Petre. If you had left us, we would have had to hide out on the mountain, and they could have attacked our family to force us to come down. So, thank you.

"But I have favor I want to ask. It is a big favor, I know. I want to leave with you. I'm not sure what I can bring, but I can help, and I will learn. Better English, yes? No problem. I will do better on my speech. If you need help in any way, I will help. I want to learn more and do more. This area is beautiful, but I want more. I wanted more before you and Nathan came. I want to learn about the Wechselbalg."

Bethany Anne considered the earnest woman. "You realize you could have died today with Petre? Not every vampire or Were we fight is going to be so easily distracted by an amazing pair of breasts." Bethany Anne grinned, and Ecaterina blushed a little.

"It often works. Men never get over them from baby to coffin, yes? Unless they like men, then I have Nathan flash them, right?"

Bethany Anne burst out laughing, imagining Nathan in the forest rubbing his nipples at a gay vampire coming out of the tunnel. That made Ecaterina start laughing too, and they fueled each other's mirth for a solid two minutes, tears streaming down their cheeks imagining the big, strong Mr. Lowell tweaking his nipples and blowing kisses at a vamp.

Finally, Bethany Anne covered Ecaterina's mouth and told her to stop laughing. She was starting to cramp. They finally faded to chuckles and wiped tears off their faces.

"I honestly don't know where we're going next, Ecaterina. We probably have to deal with this pack here in Brasov, and have Nathan find out what's on those laptops. I didn't get much from

Petre, even though he lasted longer than I would have given him credit for. I'm hoping we find something to go on because I don't want to continue doing this blind. I'm behind the other side by a good margin, and I have many more questions than answers. You could die tomorrow if you stay with me. Are you okay with that? I can give you a couple of days to think about it if you want. But asking to be with me as a part my group, under my protection, is a lifetime commitment. Others will know you chose a side that most of the world doesn't know exists. There won't be an option to opt-out, to quit once you're on my team."

To her credit, Ecaterina didn't just blurt out an answer but paused to think about the possible ramifications to her life. She felt comfortable that Bethany Anne wouldn't mind-wipe her if she declined, but this was a path to the outside, and to knowledge of people no one else here knew about. An opportunity to see the world, and if it was going to be a short ride, it would be one full of experiences she craved and answers to questions she hadn't known existed a week before. She knew Nathan had reservations about Bethany Anne, but she had none. She didn't have any preconceived notions of vampires, so Ecaterina just went on what she had seen for herself in her interactions with Bethany Anne.

Besides, how could you not love a vampire who had such a wonderful laugh?

Bethany Anne sat back in her chair. She wasn't going to rush Ecaterina's decision. If Ecaterina wanted more time, she could have it. She didn't need to know until they were ready to leave Brasov, and that wasn't happening today. She did wonder what was going through her mind. The way Ecaterina had taken out Petre had sealed the deal for Bethany Anne. Ecaterina could come along if she wanted to. Nathan would be a very happy guy, and

Bethany Anne knew that was playing a part in Ecaterina's considerations.

Personally, she wished they would just do the horizontal mambo and get it over with. It was obvious that they liked each other. For once Ecaterina had found someone she was interested enough in that she worried about getting his attention, and Nathan didn't want to scare her away by coming on too strong.

Those two were going to provide more than an ample number of opportunities for mischief in the future. She hoped they got a chance to enjoy life together.

She couldn't see the future, but she knew she had some tasks to accomplish. The local issues, of course, plus it was time to contact Frank and get him involved. Then they needed to acquire access to the funds and accounts she knew about, which would involve a trip to Switzerland or maybe Germany. Michael had a child in Germany, so she would probably choose Switzerland for her first foray into the banks. Nathan had to deal with his own interests, as well. She couldn't just keep him as a pet. Well, she *could*, but she had come to enjoy his company and his input and it wouldn't be fair. He was an important contact in the Were community, and she was about to completely upset the strictures the UnknownWorld had lived within for centuries. That alone would cause all sorts of problems. People, and she was using that term very loosely, did not like it when their comfortable understanding and place in the world was upset.

Bethany Anne got up from the table. She needed to get herself clean and go shopping. She would use some of the money Nathan had taken from Petre's house to get herself some clothes that fit appropriately. She didn't know if Brasov had a fashionable shoe store, but she hoped no ladies were wearing a pair of Christian Louboutin size sevens on her way to the store. She didn't need that kind of temptation right now.

She heard Nathan come out of the downstairs shower. It was

time he made himself useful and went with Bethany Anne to the appropriate fashionable stores available in Brasov. Bethany Anne was on a mission to buy a new wardrobe, and she spared a moment to pity any fool who got in her way.

FINIS

QUEEN BITCH

The Story Continues with book 2, *Queen Bitch*.

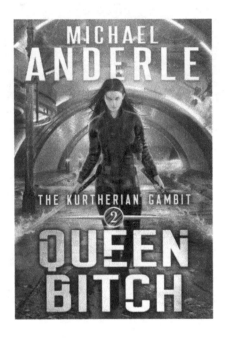

Available now at Amazon and on Kindle Unlimited

ALSO AVAILABLE IN AUDIO

The *Kurtherian Gambit* Series is also available in audio. The entire series is available as unabridged audiobooks narrated by the wonderful Emily Beresford.

Get your copy at Amazon or Audible!

The series is also available as a full cast audio recording with cinematic sound effects from Graphic Audio.

AUTHOR NOTES: MICHAEL ANDERLE

Thank you, I cannot express my appreciation enough that not only did you pick up this book, but you read it all the way to the end and NOW you're reading this as well!

I love to read. I have ever since I was in elementary school. I would have to admit that my reading got a tremendous boost due to how often I was grounded. My parents didn't believe that television or visiting friends were options while grounded.

I got grounded often. It was so bad that one time I was running neck-and-neck in a reading competition in homeroom class at school simply because I was grounded and there was nothing else I could do.

The only kind of friends I could invite over were The Three Investigators.

I found their stories exciting, their special clubhouse in the junkyard amazing, and the secret candy-in-the-globe so creative I tried to make one for myself. This was probably second or third grade. After destroying my mother's globe, one she'd had since (I think) her high school years, I found out that my imagination wasn't sufficient to overcome my lack of craft skills.

To this day I still read a lot. It is my way of disengaging my mind and traveling through someone else's exciting adventures.

My writing is escapist. I love a good action story, but more than that I want to engage with the characters. I want to feel what they're going through, if possible. I want situations that make me excited, worried, where I laugh and say "Take that, sucka!" out loud.

The challenges faced by the protagonists don't have to be life-threatening, it could be a challenge to ask that special someone out for a date that keeps the story flowing. I'm not really into books that keep you constantly afraid for the characters. If I care about a character, I'll turn the page, and buy the next book just to see them reach a personal milestone that is challenging to that character. However, having said all of that, action is what drives the story forward!

For the last couple of years, I've been bouncing back and forth between Urban Fantasy and Military Science Fiction with my personal reading. I decided that for my series, I wanted to merge both genres. How to accomplish this? I decided I would write a story arc that would start from a pivotal point here on Earth and take the characters through the effort to reach the stars and beyond.

There are presently thirteen titles* sketched out. *Death Becomes Her* (originally titled "Death Comes") is the first in the series and the next has the working title "Queen Bitch."

My thought behind Bethany Anne's character was "what happens when you take a person overly sensitive to injustice and give her the ability to kick ass and ignore the names?" I'm sure she could effect change, but it doesn't automatically follow that it will be *good* change. The fight she has might not be with another character at the end of each book, but rather with herself. Will she become that which she loathes? Will she be able to recognize the humanity in enemies, or will she become desensitized as Michael did? How will her friends react if that occurs?

Bethany Anne has a lot on her plate. Where is Michael? Is he alive? Is Carl alive? If she changes Michael's strictures that everyone follows, what happens? How does she go about dealing with the challenge to Michael with the vampire serum? Without Michael, there's a vacuum at the top of the UnknownWorld, and Bethany Anne is smart enough to know she cannot allow that to occur. She's going to need to step in and "put her size-seven Christian Louboutins" up their asses if they don't get in line.

Well, let's be real. She'll change her shoes, then implement the attitude adjustments.

That's what she's up against, so what does she have? Well, wonderful new skills. The ability to bitch-slap with the best of them. Nathan is a solid computer security wizard, and she has TOM, and the organic computer in her mind (I hope that ends up well for her).

Michael has provided some funds that she needs to access. I'm unsure what she will do for a home. Can she utilize Michael's home in New York? If she can't, where will she establish her base of operations? Will Bethany Anne ever have a romantic interest? I'm not sure.

What I have learned writing this book (other than that Scrivener is the best software for an author like me to get a book completed) is that the characters write their own stories. An example is that I didn't have Ecaterina in my story; she just tagged along. I tried to outline this story a long time ago, but I failed miserably. What worked was sitting down and writing. Hopefully, it was a fun story!

Please, if you enjoyed this book, give it a rating on Amazon. Your kind words and encouragement help any author. I will continue to the next story whether you provide an OUTSTANDING review or not, but it might get done a wee bit faster with the encouragement (smile).

Want to comment on the best scene, comment, event, shoes, or gun for Bethany Anne, weapon Nathan would prefer...you name it?

Join us on Facebook:

https://www.facebook.com/TheKurtherianGambitBooks/

Want to know when the next book or major update is ready? *Join the email list here*:

http://lmbpn.com/email/

Software used to write this book is Scrivener (Windows and Mac):

https://www.literatureandlatte.com/scrivener.php

Thank you.

Michael Anderle, November 2015

* Now a total of 21 books for The Kurtherian Gambit & 4 Additional in "The Second Dark Ages." More later ;-)

*All credit for me having ANY shoe knowledge goes to my wife, who still works to provide me with even a finger's amount of fashion sense. Why she asks me to comment on her outfits in the morning still confuses me to this day.

BOOKS BY MICHAEL ANDERLE

Sign up for the LMBPN email list to be notified of new releases and special deals!

https://lmbpn.com/email/

For a complete list of books by Michael Anderle, please visit:

www.lmbpn.com/ma-books/

CONNECT WITH THE AUTHOR

Connect with Michael Anderle

Website: http://lmbpn.com

Email List: https://michael.beehiiv.com/

https://www.facebook.com/LMBPNPublishing

https://twitter.com/MichaelAnderle

https://www.instagram.com/lmbpn_publishing/

https://www.bookbub.com/authors/michael-anderle

Printed in the USA
CPSIA information can be obtained
at www.ICGtesting.com
LVHW042254230923
758652LV00006B/1011

9 781642 020182